SOMETHING SECRET

T.R. Kester

Contents:

SOMETHING SECRET

Copyright © 2017 by TR Kester

DEDICATION

For Mary Andrew (*06/07/1966 - 15/04/2016 who lost her brave fight with cancer*), Tania Linke, Kaylee, Melissa Maingard, Neil Moreton, Susan Horsnell (my wonderful editor) and Maria Merlino-Chiarolli, all of whose inspiration and unfathomable power is secret even to them.

DISCLAIMER

Edited by Word Writer Professional and Susan Horsnell.
Note about Editing -
Editors, correct and suggest
Authors, accept or reject.

"Do nothing secretly; for Time sees and hears all things and discloses all." – Sophocles

CHARACTERS

POGUE WITCHES
Aaron

Noah

Perry

Bermuda

Isadora

Shane

ROMANI COVEN
Pilar

Madelyn

Addison

Dantalian

Persia

Brady

EXTENDED FAMILY
Ravenna - *Wife of Aaron Pogue*

Connemara Penthal - *Wife of Noah Pogue*

Kathryn Penthal - *Sister of Connemara*

Andromeda Pogue (New) - *The twin sister of Bermuda, resides in Vancouver, Canada*

Mars Romani (New) - *Twin brother of Persia and Dantalian*

Serene Rein - *Step-daughter of Pilar and elf Queen of the Autumn Forest.*

GOOD WITCHES, ROMANI AND GOOD MAGICAL BEINGS

Julyanne (New) - *A powerful witch, and High Priestess of British Columbia, Canada*

The Morrígan - *An Old One who resides in The Dream/Spirit Realms*

Diana - *Goddess and lover of Julyanne*

Gaia, Rhea, Pan & Dionysus - *Deities of Earth located in Butchart Gardens*

First Nations - *Canadian aboriginals who inhabitants of the Dream Realm*

_Chief Alo - *Leader of the Omega clan*

_Proud Buck - *Chief of the Forest Clan*

_Grey-Wing - *High Chief of the Bold Clan*

Carmen Penthal - *The deceased sister witch of Connemara & Kathryn Penthal*

Aryan - *A Mongkukulam (Filipino witch) who came to be possessed by the Old One, Vesta*

Daemon - *Dream gods who preside of the Dream Realm*

_Phantasos, Morpheus & Phobetor

Tempest Pogue - *Ancestor. Grandmother of Aaron, Noah and Perry Pogue*

Philomena Beaumont - *Ancestor. Sister of Tempest, Great Aunt of Aaron, Noah and Perry Pogue*

Amethyst - *Pogue Ancestor, begins to haunt Bermuda*

Andros - *A male witch. Possesses the power of Matter Alteration, using mirrors as portals for transportation*

Atropos, Lachesis and Clotho - *Three Sisters of Fate*

Genvera - *Leader of a group of mystical Griffins*

Pridham - *A female Custodian appointed to the Pogue Family*

Renae & Basset - *Custodians appointed to the Romani Family*

Oracles of Phaedra - *A powerful trio who can foresee all*

DEMONS AND EVIL BEINGS

Paimon - *An ancient demon king, gay lover of Asmodeus and servant of Twelve Disciples of Malignant*

Dark Promise Coven - *A congregation of evil witches that follows Alera.*

_The Judges - *Evil witches turned into demons as a reward for their worship to Asmodeus*

_King Solomon - *In ancient times was a devout follower of Alera*

Asmodeus - *An ancient demon king. Entombed in ice by the goddess, Rhea*

Kamenwati/Kamen - *Powerful Nightmare Soldier & Rafaela's right-hand demon*

_ Mangiare Demons - *Specie of Nightmare Soldiers, sub-specie of Incubo*

_ Kati - *One of three Mangiare Demons in the Dream Realm*

_Laedo - *Sub-specie of Nightmare Soldiers, the name means incapacitate in Latin*

Haarlem Blackheart - *An evil pirate, whose ship is the Nautica*

Abiteth, the Devourer - *A devourer of the beautiful and light*

Slither/Sheppard Romani - *An evil Romani and brother of Pilar*

_Snake Demons - *minions of Slither*

Melpomene - *The Muse of Tragedy and seized control over Limbo*

Rasima/Ima

Morgana

Modesto Coven

BEGINNING

"**A**t the dawn of time," Maria, Queen of Good Magic spoke as she led her Ancient Histories Class through a forest, "a few million years before the time of man, the world was a lush paradise. For the record, the world is nowhere near as picturesque today."

A student queried, "You speak as though you experienced it, Miss."

Maria smiled to herself as she silently remembered her youth.

"The oceans were crystal clear and the most magnificent blue," she touched a tree trunk before gazing upward, "forests of enormous trees which appeared to touch the sky, impressive mountains and green terrains. There were creatures in this Age of the Earth and they lived in peace with one another. It would be some time before the grand scheme of good versus evil would come to this place."

A male student interrupted as he read aloud from a text book, "Twelve holy beings reigned over the world. They would become known as the Old Ones?" he finished with a query.

"That is correct Mr. Peters." Maria continued, "The six female deities were Juno, Vesta, Minerva, Ceres, Diana and Venus. The six males were Mars, Mercury, Jupiter, Neptune, Vulcan and Apollo. They occupied the monolithic castle Mauvaise. But the Old Ones did not rise to full power until the Second Age of Earth."

"In Roman mythology, they are known as Dii Consentes," said a girl.

Another student read from her textbook, "Mauvaise was thought to be swallowed by the ground when the asteroid, which wiped out the dinosaurs, hit Earth!"

"How come the Old Ones didn't exercise their power until the Second Age?" a curious student asked.

"You are correct Jericho Hershey," Maria replied. "And, for the record, not every dinosaur was killed by the asteroid. Far worse things besides Crocodiles and Alligators survived! Mr. Hershey, it was in the Second Age that the Potentate brought all its evil to this dimension!"

The topic of the Potentate wasn't explored further at this time.

"It is thought some dinosaurs mutated and became demons," revealed a student.

Another student began, "If I may, Miss, were there witches in the First Age?"

"There were no humans in the First Age," mocked a female student.

Maria quickly intervened. "That is not entirely true, Elise. The Divinita, a solitary deity who lived amongst the clouds in the skies, came to the twelve Holy Beings and asked their permission to allow a small assembly of Prognati..." She turned and studied her students before continuing, "...which in Latin translates to Offspring, to live on Earth and see if they could sustain their own life. The Divinita believed no creature faced true adversity. So, the Prognati came into being. We later dubbed them, Neanderthals, because they lacked any kind of intelligence. But, the first witches, they are an entire subject all of their own."

Maria turned away, walked on for a few moments before halting with her students stopping not far behind her. She stared into the forest and recalled the early years of her life when she was known by her proper name Juno, the Ancient Roman Goddess and one of the twelve reigning deities. A subtle breeze elevated her long hair and her eyes sparkled as something lingered behind them.

The sunlight glimmered through the foliage of the giant trees which almost touched the sky, and warmed the faces of four young women as they lay sleeping amongst the lush grass and wild flowers in a small clearing of the forest. They were naked, long blonde hair hung almost to their knees and wore trinkets around their necks hanging on threads of glittering gold string.

"After the somewhat dismal result of the Prognati," Maria narrated, "the Divinita returned to Mauvaise with its second creation, Hominis...Latin word for Human Beings. They were nameless, fascinating beings who, at the time, appeared as human as you and I. We called the couple Atarah and Eliora, the Divinita insisted on Adam and Eve. But the four other females, we gave them their names, Alkina, Coorah, Laella and Malus. The Divinita referred to them as Venefica...Latin for Witches."

A bored student queried, "and the relevance to the creation of witches is?"

"Everything!" Maria replied a little too sharply. "After the Neanderthals..." although a human loving individual, there was a lack of enthusiasm in her voice, "well put it this way, you cannot get more stupid than Cavemen. Our only request to the Divinita was they worship Terra, Nova and Acqua like we do. They are the Omordial powers above all else, they are Earth, Fire and Water. The Doe, The Dragon and The Serpent."

"Water is governed by a serpent?"

Maria spoke again with caution. "Have you ever heard of The Loch Ness Monster?"

In the middle of the four naked women was an impressive stone, which they used as their ceremonial altar, with a pentagram engraved in it. At the center of the octagonal shape was a jewel shaped egg.

13

"Universalis Solarium," Maria murmured its name. "Four points of power converging into one to create the ultimate source. The problem with great power is lack of responsibility which seems to be a common denominator amongst mortals. We never imagined that this altar would lead to something far darker than worshipping celestial power!"

The women gathered around the pentagram and assumed the four compass points North, South, East and West. Under their touch, the jewel lowered into the center of the altar and rotated before making a locking noise. Once activated, it glowed and shot a pulse of energy up into the atmosphere. Returning, the energy re-entered the jewel, cast out another pulse and created a barrier of protection around the women and their sacred circle.

"Sun of day," the women chanted with their arms elevated toward the sky, "moon of night, hear our words, our power and might..."

"You're never supposed to look into the jewel," Maria began again, "But, Malus did."

A student queried, "Why?"

Maria continued, "In our time, we respected the higher power. The Jewel was a gift from the Divinita, a faceless deity. Even to us, it always concealed its identity; hidden beneath a white hooded cloak. To this day, it's a debated subject, whether or not the Divinita is a male or female. When the Divinita came to us, it declared...."

In the impressive Mauvaise Castle, the Divinita, hidden beneath its heavenly robes appeared before the colossal figures who were far greater in size when compared to its human six feet tall measurement.

"The Universalis Solarium Jewel is a gift from me," the voice was clear but gentle beneath its cloak, "a conduit of celestial energy. From the Venefica, every good witch on Earth and

descendant of the sisters; will be given their abilities as a divine source."

Maria spoke with a disheartened tone for a moment. "Mortals only renew their faith under dire circumstances, as though it will change the outcome for them." She then continued to narrate the story of the origins of the first good witches and evil witch, "The sisters were supposed to listen, *not* look into the scrying stone. For some time, unknown to her sisters, Malus had been listening to the whispers of a foreign entity from another dimension posing as the Divinita; it had been asking her to grant it passage into this world."

A student queried, "Because evil requires an invitation, permission to grow?"

"In theory," Maria replied.

Malus' blonde hair turned black and she was expelled from the sacred circle. She killed her sisters and became the first evil witch. Rewarded for their services of good, they were reborn from Zeus and Themis, and became known as the deities of Fates; Atropos, Clotho and Lachesis.

"Malus," Maria drew her narration to a close, "became known as Malice. For a million years, or so it seemed, we lived in peace during the Old Age. Malice brought the Potentate into this dimension and the Second Age began - the Age of Demons. Our paradise became an eternal hell!"

Chapter One

DARK PROMISE PEOPLE

The temperate Canadian forest of Ladysmith, on Vancouver Island, was beautiful and tranquil with the winter drizzle. It was hard to grasp such a place could exist and yet be uninhabited by humans. In the middle of the evergreen trees, the Haus of Romani crypt appeared gothic with its hooded statues, but rustic with its timber and yet otherworldly, thanks to the moss gave it the feel of a structure time had forgotten.

"Come to me," a woman's voice drifted on the wind, "child, I will grant you a wish..."

Stepping out of the Romani Crypt, Shane walked quickly as he glanced over his shoulder with a nervous expression on his face. Ahead of him, an abundance of black mist quickly gathered and an enchanting woman took form, clad in tattered garments.

"Come to me child, I promise you this..." Turning his attention to the area ahead of him, Shane halted abruptly as the woman placed her hands on either side of his head. "I will give you a dream you cannot refuse!"

He cried out and fell limp in her arms. Carefully she laid him on the ground and stood over him, admiring the prize she had effortlessly procured.

"That was easy," she smiled to herself.

She stood for a while longer, looking over the young witch. Her long black hair gave emitted a slight glow and a pair of long gazelle horns emerged followed by a smaller set of horns which protruded from her forehead. Her black cloak transformed into a fantastic gown. Her hair danced in a breeze, she grinned confidently and her eyes became consumed with black for a moment.

"How did you," said a female voice, "enter our realm?!"

Startled slightly, the woman's eyes returned to normal and she acknowledged the three beings standing opposite her but some distance away.

She spoke egotistically, "so you're the infamous Morrígan?" Eyeing the trio of Romani-look-a-likes up and down, she believed her power rivalled even theirs. "Trust me when I say, you are not even on the same level as me!" They gave her sour stares. "I know a trick or two about creating bridges to other dimensions. I am a Demigoddess! Now f-f," showing a bit of integrity she refrained from swearing, "fly off!"

"What do you want with the Mischling?" asked the Persia Romani look-a-like.

The woman replied, pointing where Shane lay at her feet. "This boy, is a Mischling?" She looked down at him with a smirk of curiosity, "fancy that."

The Mars Romani look-a-like spoke, "the Romani side of the witch is yet to be activated. Therefore, he is only a Mischling in theory."

"Who are you?" the Dantalian Romani look-a-like queried,

The woman's presence began to make the ground around her turn black as the evil in her sucked the goodness and life from the earth. Leaves began to float down, a few to begin with and then many soon after. The evergreen trees had begun to wither and die.

"I am Rafaela." She placed her hands on her hips and smirked. "Avatarian Demigoddess from the hell world, Alestra." Her eyes became consumed with black again and her voice deepened with power. "And this, this world - Earth, will be mine once I eradicate every bit of good."

The three spoke as one, "we're an Old One. Be careful who you choose to challenge, because there are far greater powers in this world. Powers which rival even yours, hell goddess."

"My mother was the most powerful evil witch." Ego and pride swam in her eyes as the light reflected from them. "Throughout multiple centuries she brought about terror. You've probably heard of her - *Alera*?"

The Morrígan glanced at each other knowingly. They knew the witch Rafaela spoke of; she was a prominent power in the ancient times. On occasion King Solomon had sought her out to help in the creation of his Grimoire of black magic known as the Lesser Key of Solomon.

~*~

Jerusalem, B.C...

*U*nder the full moon, a figure moved fluidly along the dirt streets of the historic town of Israel. It remained close to the shadows of the mud brick buildings, avoiding the moonlight as much as possible to prevent being noticed. Halting at a corner, it turned its head, revealing a set of vibrant red eyes from beneath its baggy hood.

It made an irritable hiss at the presence of a priest as he exited the local church. Waiting until the priest had returned to his home next door, the hooded figure moved across the street and down a dark lane between two buildings.

Entering into a mud brick house, the hooded figure stood in a room full of warm golden light, created by the flames dancing in the fireplace. The door slowly shut behind it.

It spoke, "make yourself known to me, witch." The voice was deep with power.

Behind the ominous individual, the surface of the ceiling to floor mirror mounted on the wall, rippled. A woman dressed in rags, a mop of black hair fastened up on top of her head, stepped into the room.

She spoke in a calm voice, "Hello, Solomon."

With a gesture of her elevated hand, the watery surface of the mirror behind her, magically became solid on her command. Revealing his own identity, King Solomon lowered the hood of his cloak. He had pale white skin, a bald head and noticeable vibrant red colored eyes. His fingernails were black, noticed when he freed hands from his sleeves.

"I have come," his voice was deep and imposing, "for the Grimoire, Alera."

She smiled, her eyes sparkled in the light and she crossed the room to stop and stand opposite him. Her lips pursed

"You do not intimidate me in the slightest, my dark lord." The two of them exchanged a stern glare. "I have dealt with much more powerful forces of evil, than yourself. One of them is I; you haven't seen the kind of power I possess so be careful when you see fit to challenge me. And, as for sending the demon, Asmodeus to try and kill me to gain the Lesser Key... well." She smirked as she turned her head toward the mirror. A handsome man stared back at her. "Put it that way, I took necessary precautions." Alera turned her attention back to King Solomon as the demon, Asmodeus, silently bashed on the mirror from inside his prison. "You can have your Grimoire. But I remind you firmly, do not rush me. I am not the kind of witch who gives up the ghost at the first failure. You might be King of this town, but you certainly do not possess any kind of power which warrants I should respect you in any form."

Irritably, Solomon roared, "WHERE IS THE BOOK, WITCH?"

Heavy shadows filled the room and the glow of the fire dissipated as Alera exercised her power effortlessly. Solomon contorted as immense pain suddenly overcame his body, rendering him unable to respond.

"Your grimoire is in your chambers. Now disappear." With a snap of her hand, she made him disappear in a cloud of black smoke. "As for you," she turned toward the mirror on the wall, "you can have your freedom, Asmodeus."

Swaying her arm, she gestured her hand and magically the surface of the mirror rippled. A towering man stepped through the portal into the small mud brick house.

"I have a mission for you," she explained.

He replied, "Go on."

"There is another like me in this derelict city," she spoke with repulsion.

He nodded. "She is also a witch? The one name Lindsay Hogue?"

She spoke irritably, "Yes, but she is good to my evil. You're a powerful demon, conniving too. Kill her for me, I will reimburse you with power." she smiled.

He smirked at her comment about being reimbursed for his time and then he was gone, disappearing in the blink of an eye.

~*~

*I*n the house of Lindsay Hogue, a beautiful red haired woman in her mid-thirties fell to the floor dead. Lying on her side, her eyes were still. A trickle of blood ran over her forehead and down the middle of her face.

Gathering her coven - 'The Dark Promise' in her home, to celebrate the death of the good witch, Alera suddenly fell to the floor dead; suffering the same wounds as Lindsay.

Somehow without even realizing, their lives were linked to one another. The myth began from here of two witches, 'The Yin and the Yang'. The good witch in the evil witch and the evil witch in the good witch.

With the evil witch's demise, King Solomon assumed leader of the Dark Promise Coven in Jerusalem until his own fate was decided. Vaticus O'Preach, a follower of Alera assumed leadership of the evil coven of witches before relocating it when word of a child named Jesus, a powerful force of good far greater than the evil of the coven, was born in Bethlehem.

Like Treadwell, Deane County, Jerusalem was built upon a Leviathan.

"It is the duty of Witches and Slayers, to protect the Hell Mouths around the world," the female Morrígan proclaimed with a profound sense of knowledge. "The Divinita sent down the Leviathan from the heavens. They were one of its first creations, and far too powerful to be controlled so, they were sent to Earth. Embedded in the ground, we Old Ones built our Parthenon's upon them. First, we constructed Mauvaise, but then erected many more to disguise them from evil."

The Morrígan who resembled Mars Romani spoke, "When the first evil witch, Malus, brought evil into this dimension via the Universalis Solarium and the Age of Demons began, the Divinita watched the Potentate and its forces conquer many of our Parthenons. Many demons, and evil Old Ones, gained significant strength through these occupations and proceeded to use them as portals to and from the Underworld to help trapped creatures escape."

The Morrígan who resembled Dantalian Romani continued, "The Leviathans slowly became linked to one another, acting as portals between the two worlds of Hell and Earth. They also radiate power, drawing either good or evil to them. Cities like Treadwell, Vancouver, New York, New Orleans, Salem, Jerusalem and

Sunnydale, California to mention a few, were created to contain the power of the Hell Mouths and prevent an apocalypse of any magnitude."

Rafaela rolled her eyes, moved her head and expelled a pulse of energy out of irritation.

"Be quiet." She directed her glare at the three figures. "Seriously, I do not need a pep talk from the spirit of an Old One. My mother, Alera came to Jerusalem from Babylon to defeat that bitch Lindsay Hogue, the Warden of the Hell Mouth. But, then it came to light, she was the Evil to the Good of that red-haired harlot. Neither one could exist without the other."

"Some legends are best left dead and buried," the Morrígan said firmly in unison as they silently read the demigoddesses aura. "Leave this realm or we will remove you by force."

Rafaela strengthened her dark stare, her aura ignited ferociously with black energy, the sky above became a heavy grey as thunder and lightning manifested from her rage.

~*~

Working her way through the forest, Kathryn Penthal encountered a wide tree. The ground was covered in pine needles, nurse trees, branches and moss. Touching the trunk of the evergreen in front of her, it glowed and she vanished in a smoky wisp. Reappearing in another wisp, she found herself inside the Haus of Romani.

"Where?" she murmured in disbelief. "What is this place?"

It was dark and dirty, a distinct smell of stale air wafted about her as though the place had not been open in centuries. Peering at the window, she noted daylight behind it and then sudden flashes. A loud explosion of thunder resonated close by; startled, she gasped and looked toward the open door.

Halting at the door, she pulled it inward slightly and caught a glimpse of the outside. In a clearing, Rafaela stood proud and dark, Shane Penthal lay at her feet.

"Shane," Kathryn gasped softly,

Observing the confrontation from behind, she was able to identify three ghostly figures. Two male and a female stood opposite the evil demigoddess.

"You cannot remove me," Rafaela yelled and the ground shook. "You cannot remove us." Struck by lightning, using her own evil magic, four ghostly figures extended from her body. "We are the promise people, the promise of great things and power."

Four cloaked individuals stood behind Rafaela. Their presence overwhelmed the forest to the point of amplifying the demigoddesses' power. Her poisonous black quickly spread out and withered the beauty of the dimension.

"The Dark Promise Coven," Rafaela spoke arrogantly and with a smirk of confidence, "meet the Morrígan, the Old One and creator of the Romani. Morrígan, meet the Judges - Nord, Sud, Est and Ovest."

Elevating their hung heads, ram horns extended from beneath their hoods and vibrant red eyes shone in an attempt to intimidate the Old One.

The Morrígan spoke in unison, "Evil witches turned into demons as a reward for their worship to Asmodeus."

Rafaela replied happily, "Thanks to my husband."

She revealed the demon, Asmodeus, was in actual fact her husband. Many centuries later Alera's fourth reincarnation manifested in Istanbul, Turkey in 1940, still going by the same name and still every bit as evil. She had a daughter named, Rafaela, to the demon Ruskav Des Krute. But, in this life-time something was different. She and Lindsay Hogue occupied the same body making killing one, and it not affecting the other, impossible.

The secret to their demise in this life came when local monks, of the *'Holy Grace'* parish, devised a theory. By binding one of the witches' powers, they were capable of weakening the other in order to vanquish Alera, which unfortunately resulted in Lindsay's death also.

But, just like every life she had lived and died in before, Alera resurrected the Dark Promise Coven. However, this time, for her servitude, Asmodeus asked for her daughter Rafaela to be his bride to concentrate the evil between the friends.

~*~

Extending her arms to the sky, Rafaela called for the thunder.

Drawing her arm down with her hand gestured, she magically brought down bolts of lightning which struck the ground around her vigorously. Opening her hands, she drew the lightning from the ground and into her grasp, turning it black in color.

"Let me show you." Her evil smile was beautiful. "...how to remove something unwanted!"

Reaching her arms forward, she released the lightning she had conducted in her hands and projected it at the Old One.

Extending one arm each, a hand gestured at the Avatarian Demigoddess, the Morrígan displayed their great power even though they were in mere spirit form. Rafaela's lightning evaporated and let out a scream as energy rippled around her, and her Dark Promise followers, before causing them to explode into a black mist. The mass shot backward, taking with it the black which had reached through the forest, then disappeared in a quick flash of light. Effortlessly, Rafaela and her followers, had been banished from the dimension.

Witnessing it all, Kathryn gulped nervously before exiting the Romani Crypt.

"Shane," she called.

Nervously, she made eye contact with The Morrígan as she passed them, fearing the same fate would befall her. They stared at her cautiously, not knowing exactly what her nature was. But after a moment of secretly reading her aura, they exuded a more content expression on their faces and allowed her to tend to the unconscious witch.

~*~

Down in the depths of the Underworld, in her marvelous lair, Rafaela was thrown back into her throne as she disconnected from the crystal ball sitting on a pillar in front of her. She had used it to Astral Project into the overlapping Dream and Spirit Realms.

"Ugh," she grumbled as she composed herself, "That was not what I was expecting. How was that possible?" she turned toward her oracle; a beautiful woman with blue hair. "The Old One banished me and the coven. It was a stupid spirit; you told me. The Morrígan possessed no power because it was supposed to be dead." Rafaela's voice dripped with anger.

"Forgive me my Liege," the nervous Oracle replied.

MEET ME IN NANAIMO
PART 1

The wind howled through the inlet between Protection Island and Newcastle Island Park on the snowing winter's night in the bay of Nanaimo, on Vancouver Island. The glow of the full moon peeked out from behind the clouds and danced across the water for a second before disappearing again.

In that second, it outlined a black robed figure walking on the surface of the ocean. Peeking out from behind the clouds again, the light captured four other robed figures as they rose up from beneath the water's surface and began following ten paces behind the figure in front.

The evil presence of the Dark Promise Coven caused the water beneath them to freeze. Approaching the shore, the five figures were noticed by a man and a woman who were collecting driftwood. With a brisk gesture of its hand, the figure in front turned the innocent mortals to solid ice; killing them instantly.

Rafaela cast her summoning spell from beneath the hood of her robe. "Howling wind, we call thee. Bring us to he, king of the demons, Paimon."

Magically the wind whipped around the five figures and teleported them away.

~*~

While the icy, winter winds blew outside, inside a bar in the Old Nanaimo quarter of the city, innocent mortals socialized and drank alcoholic beverages. The Provincial, an up-market, French inspired salon was a place of expensive taste. Rich business men, high profile women and young self-possessed socialites were common here.

The walls were a moody purple with black leather booths and dark timber tables. In the middle of the club, raised above the patrons, was a square stage where a girl band in grey cocktail dresses performed the song *Sledgehammer* by *Fifth Harmony*.

Occupying a booth in the far corner of the bar, sat a charming man. He wore a suit with a satin finish, drank a dirty martini and looked as though he fitted comfortably into the forty something age bracket. The moody atmosphere made his square cut jaw, and perfectly quaffed salt and pepper hair, more alluring. His eyes were an interesting shade of purple.

Sitting on the end of the circular booth, he had conveniently filled every other position with gorgeous women who laughed at his jokes, sighed in awe of his smile and fell into lust by the simple bat of his eyelashes. Clearly this man was not human, because women do not behave this way with any average guy, unless she thinks she can gain something.

~*~

One hour prior...

A beguiling blonde haired, young woman walked along Front Street, Nanaimo, making her way to the Provincial Bar. Her long hair was pulled back in a ponytail which hung over her shoulder; she *wore an alluring dress and designer stilettos. The light captured her green eyes as she cautiously moved her gaze about the street. Approaching the French inspired entrance of the bar, she released her hair, ruffled it with her hand and stared at the guard at the door.*

"Andy," she spoke her name in her Australian accent, "Andy Pogue."

The male looked her up and down. Mesmerized by her eyes, he suddenly became entranced as a subtle glow flashed from them. Holding her hand out, she blew a gentle breath and magically enchanted him by casting sparkling pink fairy dust into his face. The moment she disappeared from his sight, he had no recollection of ever seeing her.

Sipping her Cosmopolitan cocktail at the Bar, the enchantress, Andy Pogue observed the performing act. To each side of her men and women flirted with one another as they exited the weekly grind of their nine to five jobs and began to relax into the weekend. The seat beside her vacated as a gentleman escorted a female out of the bar. Just as quick, the seat was reoccupied when a woman sat down.

"Hello," the woman indirectly greeted Andy Pogue in a formal manner. "Andromeda Pogue. You're a very long way from Treadwell."

Turning her head, and swivelling her body in the seat, Andy Pogue looked at the person who had spoken, and appeared to know her. Startled, she coughed as she choked for a moment on her beverage.

"High Priestess Webb," she greeted the woman curiously, "Wh–what are you doing here?"

The mature aged woman dressed in a thick knitted, cream colored cardigan over an ash grey satin dress, with shoulder length salt and paper hair flicked her fingers at the bartender.

"Whiskey?" she asked. "Please." Turning her focus back to Andy Pogue, the woman continued. "This is my jurisdiction, dear, so I will ask the questions when I suspect good witches are up to no good." Andromeda gave a reluctant stare. "Ms. Pogue, I don't want trouble in my quarters. Please tell me," she took a sip of her whiskey, "your tactics for your unanticipated visit."

"Evil," Andromeda announced.

Her particular wording came as the entrance door blasted opened and a gust of icy wind blew in as a heavily cloaked figure entered. The flow of time immediately stood still.

Fog swept across the floor as five figures entered the bar, and threaded their way through the shocked mortals to the back, where the gentleman sat in his booth.

"ID," summoned the guard at the door when the figures approached. "I cannot let you without ID."

"Be silent," Rafaela began to rhyme, "be still, be frozen, I kill!"

Before him, five dark and heavily cloaked figures stood, their faces unseen. With a brisk wave of her hand, leader, Rafaela from beneath her cloak turned the man at the door into a solid ice sculpture.

Andromeda was unable to be frozen in time by the presence of the evil, Dark Promise Coven. Her eyes gave off a subtle green glow for a moment and she was released by the power which entrapped everyone else in the bar.

"High Priestess Webb." She waved her hand in the face of the woman sitting beside her. "Julyanne? ...Shit."

Not everyone great and powerful is immune to the power of Molecular Manipulation, otherwise known as Eloquence - the ability to stop the flow of time.

Andromeda had in her possession a talisman of a crescent moon which granted her immunity to multiple powers.

Taking a deep breath, she composed herself while quickly glancing about the immediate area. She then used her power of Invisibility to disappear.

~*~

In almost an elegant manner, the five cloaked figures moved like silk on a breeze across the floor. Rafaela halted before the charming gentleman and removed her hood to reveal her face and horns. Merely pretending to be still, far more powerful than expected, the gentleman moved and his eyes met the demigoddesses. They exchanged a challenging glare.

"Pray tell," he growled, took a sip of his beverage and his eyes gave off a glow, "*hell-spawn*. What is it you want?" Looking her over and silently acknowledging the figures behind her, he continued, "Rafaela and the Dark Promise Coven, I presume? Your reputation precedes you."

Appearing human in visage on the outside, although pure demon inside, Rafaela gave the man a humble smile. He wasn't fooled; he knew it was nothing but a sly gesture.

"Paimon." She spoke his name with an ego driven tone. "The ancient and powerful."

He retorted with vicious sarcasm, "Don't forget *royal*, missy."

Without a care for the intimidation the coven tried to present, Paimon took a sip of his dirty martini. He placed the glass down on the table and re-engaged eye contact with Rafaela.

"I grow bored." He lifted his eyebrows before narrowing his eyes impatiently. "What is it you want, Avatarian? Tell me, before I get up and leave... you're ruining my night!" Turning his head, he observed the women in his company before focusing on Rafaela again.

"You're a demon king of many teachings; reveal many mysteries about the Earth, Wind and Water, the mind and what the Conjurer wants to know." His stare was cold toward her and he peered down his nose, he didn't need a reminder.

"So, I request..."

Abruptly, he attempted to teleport from the bar in a swirl of grey smoke but was rendered unable. Elevating her hand, she revealed a Babylon crystal with an inverted pentagram symbol engraved in it.

"I know your weakness. I found a Babylon Crystal. You're unable to leave until I get what I want, understand?"

He replied coldly, "loud and clear."

She revealed her intention and why she had travelled to the dimension. "I tried to retrieve a minion of mine from the Dream Realm. I almost had a Pogue Witch in my possession but unfortunately, I unexpectedly encountered The Morrígan whose power outweighed even mine and the coven. It banished us."

Paimon smirked. "You tried to sustain longevity in a realm heavily powered by Aboriginals, what did you expect?"

"Aboriginals?" she queried with confusion,

"First Nations, American Indians, Australian Dream Time People etc..." Paimon studied her, pondering her level of intelligence, or if she was in fact a rather stupid individual without any carnal knowledge. "You have been around long enough to know evil cannot sustain a long-term life form in that dimension. Only Incubo Nightmare Soldiers, Incubi and Succubi can because of their ability to assume an incorporeal form. But, as for The Morrígan, that's a power even *I* do not wish to challenge. Old Ones should not be challenged, they can wipe you clean off the face of the earth with only a thought. It would be wise not to antagonize another!"

"Blah-blah, quit the small talk Casanova." She levitated the Babylon Crystal in her open hand. "Kamenwati was supposed to report back. Meet me here in Nanaimo. But, she has not shown. I instructed her to abduct Prometheus Pogue, take him to the Dream Realm and withdraw information from him in regards to resurrecting the Beast."

Paimon eyed her suspiciously. "You sent a demon into uncharted waters which are overlooked, not only by an Old One, but also powerful Daemons. Morpheus, being one of them. Chances are your minion is dead or the Filipino witches of the Mangarap Biyahero (Dream Traveller) Coven have figured out her mission and trapped her."

"Such a wealth of knowledge you possess Paimon." Rafaela smiled at the demon before her.

He sat back, displayed a smirk of intrigue and then queried, "which Beast are you intent on resurrecting?"

"Alera!"

His eyebrows rose and he sat forward with an eager look on his face, his arm waved into the air "I will assist you. Alera was the most captivating, and merciless evil presence, I ever came across in Babylon. She was a master, a beast. When she left with the ambition of taking control of the Hell Mouth in Jerusalem, I never saw her again." He emitted sparkling red energy.

Pleased by his response, Rafaela strengthened her smile. She could see her evil intentions coming to fruition sooner rather than never.

"Across the bridge, the dimension is passed." Paimon cast a summoning spell over the sparkling red energy, "bring down the veil, let my power surpass." Although invisible, Andromeda paid close attention to how the energy attracted the light in the room, causing it to become gloomy. "I call to thee, Kamenwati; your attendance belongs with me."

Before the room reached total darkness, Andromeda reached her arm out from behind a still mortal and called for the Babylon Crystal in Rafaela's possession.

"Venite ad me," (Come to me) she spoke in Latin.

In the moment from light to dark, the crystal dissolved and reformed in the palm of her open hand. As if anticipating what would happen, Rafaela gave a look of satisfaction and folded her arms.

"Where is she?" she demanded into the darkness.

Paimon clapped his hands once and the light returned with Kamenwati standing between him and the Demigoddess. Rafaela stood with her arms elevated, her hands over her face, frozen in fear as if meeting her painful demise. She was painfully gripped by the arm and Rafaela, the members of the Dark Promise Coven, and Kamenwati teleported out of the bar in a cloud of black smoke.

Time regained its momentum, the sound of people laughing and music playing returned to the quiet establishment. Rising from his comfortable booth, Paimon fixed the button of his blazer, thanked his women friends and made his way out through the back exit of the bar.

Remaining invisible, Andromeda, unsatisfied the demon Paimon had slipped from her grasp, grumbled to herself and quickly began her pursuit.

Chapter Three

MEET ME IN NANAIMO
PART TWO

The wind picked up and wailed like a banshee in snow dusted cars in the parking lot of the BC Ferries Departure Bay Terminal in Nanaimo British Columbia. Snowflakes glimmered like diamonds beneath the glow of the street lights.

Reappearing in a blur of energy, Paimon, tall and proud in his designer suit, strode toward the ferry loading ramp and the unsettled waters of the bay. He sighed before a smile formed on his smooth face as though he had achieved something great.

"Stupid girl," he murmured arrogantly to himself. "Resurrecting Alera, the nerve..." The tone of his voice revealed his true opinion of Rafaela as being an incompetent idiot, with more influence then sense. "These modern-day demons have far more arrogance then common sense. I am Paimon," he announced to the wind, to the deserted area around him which was devoid of human beings. "I am the ancient, I am..."

Ahead, dressed in winter attire, Bermuda Pogue completed an under-arm throw at her side. Her hand shone a golden color and she used her power of Deflection to throw him backwards onto the ground.

"Hello Paimon," she smiled, halting in front of him as he sat himself upright. "Remember me?" Bermuda winked one eye.

He narrowed his stare. "Bermuda Pogue."

Exploding onto his feet, he used his power of Accelerated Speed to charge at the witch in a blur of gray. Abruptly, he was halted. He groaned in discomfort as his bones creaked and moved, as though manipulated by someone other than him. Once again, his backside hit the ground.

"I believe we haven't been formerly introduced," said another voice. Andromeda stepped out of Bermuda's silhouette. "Hi. Andromeda Pogue."

Andromeda was the one using her power of Tele-Bone Manipulation to cripple him and render him immobile. She had changed from her beautiful dress, worn in the Provincial Bar, to warm winter attire like her sister.

"You," he grumbled as he climbed to his feet. With a glare on his face he revealed his knowledge of her, "You've been following me, and have been an unrelenting pain in my ass! Do you know how many demons of mine you have vanquished?"

Andromeda smirked. "I know I've not vanquished enough to satisfy my urges."

"Hmm..." He narrowed his eyes. "You're not from around here, are you? I should have known..." He used his power of Soul Reading, "You're twins!"

"No, we're not from around here. We're Treadians," hissed Andromeda.

Bermuda elevated her hand and allowed it to glow gold as she activated her power.

"Ah, not on me, you don't!" She blocked him magically, "None of that Soul Reading crap, mate. We've got plans for you."

He turned his body away slightly. "And if I decide not to comply?"

"I'm going to put your testicles in a vice." Andromeda clarified her intention with a hand gesture.

Bermuda interrupted quickly. "Enough Andy. Comply Paimon or you risk being vanquished if you don't."

Behind the demon, with a brilliant glowing aura as her power of Photokinesis absorbed the photons from the street lights, Isadora Pogue made her presence known.

"Well," she spoke, causing him to glance at her from corner of his eye, "being vanquished is inevitable. You're not a Stealth Demon, Paimon, you're just ancient. Therefore, the three of us have enough combined Pogue Power to vanquish you."

Paimon narrowed his eyes suspiciously. "You do know who, and what, I represent, right?"

The three young women gazed at him attentively.

"I'm a mere magician compared to those I speak for."

Isadora, out of irritation, maneuvered her hand, moved her arm, and projected a small beam of light at the back of his lower leg. Crying out in agony, he buckled down onto one knee.

"Cut the crap, King," she growled.

Bermuda flicked her hand in midair, requesting her sister to cease the attacks.

"We know who, and what, you speak for." She revealed confidently with a smirk of ego on her face. "At the end of the Third Age, when the Demon Old Ones and their armies fled this world upon the arrival of the asteroid, and a path for a new race of man was paved; the last twelve remaining demons who stayed behind combined their efforts to create, 'The Twelve Disciples'."

~*~

*S*ome hours prior, in an apartment on the corner of Robson and Hamilton in downtown Vancouver on the fourteenth floor of a modern glass building; Isadora, Bermuda and her twin sister Andromeda browsed through their Book of Shadows.

Raising her eyes from the pages of the family heirloom, Isadora was momentarily captivated by the twinkling lights of the Canadian city at night.

"No wonder you love it here," she expressed with infatuation. "Such beautiful and panoramic scenery you must wake up to every morning, Andy."

Andromeda elevated her face a little, brushed loose stands of blonde hair back behind her ear, and simply smiled at her younger sister's comment. She stood opposite to the kitchen counter with one hand on her hip while her other hand, traced sentences on the page in front of her.

"It says here." She read the blurb in the Book of Shadows about the demon Paimon, "Do not be persuaded by his delightful looks, Paimon is an ancient demon from Babylon before the time of Christ. He is a spokesman for The Twelve Disciples of Malignant."

Isadora queried, "Who are The Twelve Disciples of Malignant?" She lingered by the windows and gazed out over the city below.

"More like what?" Bermuda interrupted before continuing. "They a congregation of Original Demons who – when the great asteroid came and exterminated the dinosaurs, and a magic free world for man was paved and the Old Ones driven from this dimension – decided to remain in secret in the deepest part of the Underworld to govern the side of darkness."

"Paimon has the ability of Inter-Dimensional Summoning." Andromeda informed, as she pointed to his active powers written at the bottom of the page. "He is able to bring demons and figures to him from various dimensions. Or," she glanced up at Isadora before turning her attention to Bermuda, "be able to open a portal to the Dream Realm. We can use him to get there and find Noah, Perry, Shane and Kathryn."

A confident smirk rose to the surface of her face when Isadora expressed concern.

Raising her eyes from the pages of the book, an almost unnoticeable gasp slipped from Bermuda's lips as she acknowledged the presence of an invisible individual through the Mediumship branch of her Sensazione power.

"Connemara," she whispered,

Andromeda queried, "What was that, sweetie?"

A woman with long, thick dark hair raised her finger to her lips seeking quiet. In an instant, she vanished. Behind a partly opened door to a bedroom in darkness, she reappeared. Moving her head, she peered into the living area of the apartment and observed the three young women.

"Come together." The three sisters stood around the kitchen counter and cast a locator spell over a map of the province of British Columbia. "Gather around, magic forces hear us now."

Moments passed, their call for assisted magic in a foreign country was not strong enough because their lineage was connected to the powers which existed in Treadwell, Deane County.

"We have no power here, I cannot even radiate light," Isadora grumbled irritably.

Bermuda corrected, "that's not entirely true, it works on a broader scale. Our power is tied to Treadwell, and the Hellmouth. We're only restricted. We will need permission from the High Priestess, Julyanne, to have full magical access."

"We can work around her," Andromeda revealed with a sinister expression on her face. "We can use Talismans. That is how I am able to fully utilize my magic." Elevating her hand to her lips, she cast a few words, "Magic, essence, intertwine, breath of life too now combine." She blew her breath over the palm of her hand, casting glittering dust into the air.

The diamond pendant around Isadora's neck shimmered and glowed. A magic wind blew her long hair back, her indigo *colored eyes shone a bold purple. Likewise, Bermuda's green eyes shone a brilliant emerald and the teardrop jewel on a chain around her neck shimmered and glowed.*

Isadora extended her arm forward. "Find us the demon, Paimon." She used her power of Photokinesis to illuminate the map on the counter.

~*~

The wind picked up again, it howled, blowing icy snow flakes around the three witches and demon in the middle of the Departure Bay BC Ferry terminal parking lot. Rising back onto his feet, Paimon arched his back, breathed in deep and let out a roar.

Intimidated, Isadora took a step backward and quickly gathered sparkling light into the palms of her hands.

"What the hell is he doing?" she asked her sisters.

Ram horns slithered from his head, and the handsome appeal in his face quickly diminished as he assumed a demonic visage, and grew a few inches taller.

He glared down at Bermuda, "Now, do, *you*, want to beg for your life, witch?"

The sisters exchanged a hostile glare with the creature.

"Do you want to beg for yours?" Andromeda snapped nastily while revealing the Babylon Crystal in her possession. "Play nice, or I *will* make your entire existence up until now seem like heaven. I'm a woman. I know how to place a man's balls in a vice and make him scream for mercy."

Undaunted, he crouched slightly, levelled his eyes with Andromeda, and roared.

Andromeda cast a spell. "Crystal Babylon, curse of bone, vile fiend, demon Paimon, bound to thee..." The small magical crystal in her open hand, began to levitate and glow.

Threatened by the potential of the crystal, Paimon composed himself, and magically reverted back to his enchanting mortal form.

"What do you want?" he demanded.

Isadora spoke, "In exchange for your life, we want you to help us cross into the Dream Realm. And, don't say you don't know how, because we've done our research. We know you have the power to reach into dimensions and bring beings to you."

Paimon glanced at the beautiful young witch from the corner of his eye, toward Andromeda as she levitated the Babylon Crystal in her hand and noted Bermuda by her side.

"Fine," he agreed. "But, you won't find any portal to the Dream Realm here. Besides, what's in it for me?"

Isadora was quick to reply first, "Don't waste our time, you idiot. Take us to where the boundaries between the dimensions are."

Bermuda raised her hand. "Isadora, keep your Bipolar in check." She raised her eyebrows with irritation, "Paimon, our offer is immunity. We won't come after you, and you," she pointed at him with a fierce expression on her face, "don't come after us. Do we have a deal?"

Paimon looked at the crystal levitating over Andromeda's hand.

"You have a deal," he replied cautiously.

Andromeda snapped the crystal back into her hand. "Good man! Now tell us to where the dimensions cross. We know they are predominately here in the British Columbia area."

"There are dimensional rifts at Porteau Cove, Provincial Park, Pender Island, and Ladysmith. But, with the help of some garden magic, I can open a portal in Butchart Gardens," he revealed humbly.

Andromeda asked curiously, "Garden magic?"

"He is talking about Wood Nymphs," Isadora informed her sisters.

Bermuda spoke arrogantly, "we leave now."

Moving forward, Andromeda, Bermuda and Isadora placed a hand on Paimon.

"Teleportato! the Butchart Gardens!" the three girls said in sync.

Magically, in a brilliant flash of light, they teleported to their next destination. It was easier to travel via magic instead of an hour and thirty-four-minute-long drive from Nanaimo to Brentwood Bay, near Victoria, the Capitol of British Columbia.

Stepping out from behind a snow dusted car, Connemara Penthal. An ethereal woman with thick, long black hair and silver eyes with decorative crow feathers on the side of her head, had been secretly observing the three young witches since appearing to Bermuda Pogue in her sister Andromeda's apartment. She looked down her nose with despise for Paimon before magically using her Therianthrope power to shapeshift into a crow, taking flight into the wintery night.

~*~

II tell you this," Bermuda grumbled in the dark. "A Wood Nymph must be one of three things to be out in this fricken, freezing cold weather. One being a really keen gardener," the acid in her voice gave her body warmth, "two, have no feeling or three, completely frozen stiff."

Paimon's manly voice rose as the four of them walked along the dark garden path through the Butchart Botanical Gardens.

"Does she usually complain like this?"

"This is her actually being quite placid," remarked Isadora, "I dare you to get her started about characters on the television show - *The Bold and the Beautiful*."

Andromeda interrupted quickly, "It's bad enough she is complaining about the snow, Isadora, must you give her a reminder about the soap opera?"

"Oh?" Paimon asked curiously. "Pray tell."

Bermuda shrieked when she slipped in snow on the path, "it's got me."

"What's got you?" Isadora questioned impatiently.

Andromeda growled, "you've got *me*, by the arm, clearing you're not worth taking, Bermuda. You merely stepped snow in fresh snow."

Bermuda managed to correct her balance by grasping hold of Andromeda.

"You three would make bad robbers if you ever tried to burgle a place," Paimon joked to soften the sibling tension. "Being silent so you don't get caught is clearly something you're not familiar with, right?"

Ignoring the comment, Andromeda gavel the group some history of the place they found themselves in. "According to legend, Butchart Gardens was founded by Robert Pim and his wife Jennie Butchart who came here to Brentwood Bay, Vancouver Island from Owen Sound, Ontario in 1904 prior to it becoming the Sunken Garden in 1921, Robert Pim had used it as a quarry to excavate limestone for Portland cement."

Isadora asked, "According to legend or according to Wikipedia? I can see the glow of your phone from the corner of my eye, Andy."

Paimon halted, his movement abruptly causing the three sisters to crash into the back of him, Andromeda almost dropping her phone in the snow.

"God," Bermuda protested. "Give us some warning next time."

Andromeda gasped, "I almost lost my phone."

Isadora swore, "shit." But, hurriedly corrected herself, "I meant, shivers."

Paimon yelled, "Gaia!"

Bermuda whispered to her sisters, "I thought when he said Garden Magic, he meant Wood Nymphs, not the fricken Goddess of Earth."

Isadora murmured, "Okay, so maybe we got it wrong."

"Personally, I was secretly hoping for garden gnomes." Andromeda continued their whispering as she observed from the back of the group. "This just blew that theory out of the preverbal window."

Chapter Four

NINETEEN EIGHTY-EIGHT

*I*n an abyss of darkness, thunder continuously rumbled. There
were flashes of lightning, and music began to play. First there was
electro pop, up-tempo beat, then the pounding bass followed by
piano music and a chorus of women ascended the area into light.

A dance floor emerged, and the four women of HotLips,
dressed in skimpy attire and holding umbrellas, performed their
version of 'It's Raining Men'. The sounds of thunder rumbled in the
nightclub and the lighting created flashes of lightning.

The eighties were an era of sex, drugs and rock 'n' roll; music
had heart and soul, disco was losing its place in the world.

It was a Saturday night and 'Temptation', one of Treadwell's
lucrative clubs, was in full throttle party mode. On the dance floor,
in front of the performing act, Perry Pogue showed off his smooth
moves as he danced with a leggy, dark-haired woman. She had
been around for a while, and for him, that was something
significant. The youngest of the Pogue Brothers did not keep a
woman for longer than a few days.

Some hours later, in the moonlight of his dark bedroom,
Perry and his date, lay on his bed and engaged in a heated make
out session which could only lead to one thing. Shirtless, he lay on
top of her with one of her legs elevated and wrapped around his
behind. His hand was firm against the silky skin of her thigh. Her
head was angled slightly to the side of his as it rested on the pillow.
She arched her back and gasped with every kiss he placed against

her neck. Their pleasure rose with either one's touch on each other's body.

Hungry for the next stage, Perry rose to his knees as she unfastened and removed her bra. He lunged down and began to kiss and fondle her chest. Straightening up, he remained kneeling over her, and gestured his hand at the nightstand. A condom, still in its wrapper, floated into his hand with the aid of his power of Telekinesis.

"I want you," he announced lustfully.

As she sat up and unfastened his belt and zipper, she replied, "Take me, I want you Perry."

The morning dawned, as it always did after every encounter between them, and she would sneak out of the bed, grab her possessions and leave before he awoke. Theirs, had been a secret rendezvous for the past twelve months. Her husband at home was none-the-wiser about their affair.

~*~

*T*hree weeks passed, and she made no contact. He would keep his distance, knowing too well the repercussions if her husband discovered her infidelity.

It was a sunny day on Hastings Beach in the western suburbs of Treadwell, the waves rolled onto the golden sand. With his tank-top tucked into his shorts, Perry, sweaty and panting, was on his usual jog. He had the earphones of his Sony Walkman in his ears and was oblivious to everything around him.

"Perry," called a voice, lost on the wind as music blasted in his ears.

As he jogged closer, a woman waved him down. Slowing to a walk before halting, he removed his earphones and pressed pause on his music device. He ran his hand through his sweaty hair, caught his breathe and smiled at the couple in front of him.

"Perry," his sister-in-law flashed him her beautiful smile. "How are you? Fancy seeing you down here, do you come down to Hastings often?"

"Hi, sorry. I didn't see you until you waved. Yeah, I come down here every day for my jog."

"Sorry, mate." He wiped his sweaty hand on his shorts and shook his brother's hand. "How are you?"

The husband replied, "How are you? Good weather for the beach."

"Yeah, great weather and I'm good thanks. We'll have to get together soon."

"Anyway, I must be going." Wanting to avoid further, awkward conversation, he placed his earphones back in his ears and started to walk off. "It was nice running into you, see you soon. Give me a call."

Glancing over his shoulder, Perry looked back and watched them walk away down the beach.

He talked to himself as his eyes panned the scenic view around him, "You're an idiot Perry."

~*~

*T*he same night, there was a knock on Perry's front door.

Standing on the front porch as it poured with rain, the woman gave him a comforting smile. Thunder rumbled in the night.

"I wasn't sure," she spoke carefully. "I wasn't sure if you were home."

Perry replied, "What game are we playing here? You're married, do I need to remind you? You only come looking for me when you want to F..., when you want to feel something that isn't your husband between your legs." He refrained from swearing, even though the word he was going to use was exactly what they did whenever the two came together. "

She slapped him hard across the face. Although discouraged by his honesty, the woman remained silent before her lips formed a slight smile. She seemed to understand the hardness of Perry's position. He wanted something different to what she was proposing, but what he wanted, she got from her husband and she was not prepared to sacrifice. What they had was sex with no strings attached.

They stared at one another for what seemed like a long time as both struggled to find mutual ground or understanding. But finally, he caved in.

"Stuff it." Reaching forward, he pulled her toward him.

She smirked, leapt up onto his hips and wrapped her legs around his waist. They began to make out passionately, right there on the front porch for the whole world to see.

Turning around, Perry staggered back inside and slammed the door shut behind them.

~*~

*A*nother three weeks passed, the woman kept her distance again and he could not figure out why. But, preparing to leave for America to take up a lucrative position in New York Fashion Week, and possibly live there permanently, Perry was confronted by his love at Treadwell Airport.

Unafraid of the exposure of magic, the woman boldly stopped the flow of time. The employee behind the check-in desk stood still, her jaw in an awkward position, frozen whilst talking. Cautious, Perry looked the clerk over and turned his head, noticing *every other mortal around him was still. Looking a little further, he saw the woman was dressed in denim shorts, a nice blouse and long knitted cardigan which hung just above her ankles. She was stunning.*

"Are you fricken nuts?" he growled at her. He assumed his vampire face for a second before returning to his mortal appearance. "You're going to expose us and the magic."

She questioned him, "Why are you leaving?"

He revealed the truth of his departure. "I've been offered a place in New York Fashion Week. I won't be returning. But, why are you really here? We need to put an end to this."

The mood between them was somber, he had his reservations about seeing her, and she didn't want to see him go. Their relationship was like a forbidden fruit they kept coming back to taste, and indulge in. knowing only too well, the toxicity it possessed. With a gesture of her hand at her side, she allowed time to resume itself.

She asked, "This? What is this?"

"Us," he replied, curiously noticing her hand resting on her stomach. "This, whatever this is. I don't want to continue being the other man. You have a husband and you need to consider him in this. If you love me, let me go, because I have let you go. It pains me, but I need to leave this place. Leave Treadwell and start a new life for myself."

She looked at him calmly.

He moved his eyes from where her hand rested over her stomach, "I doubt you're here to try and stop me from leaving. Am I right?"

Her expression became unreadable.

"I'm pregnant Prometheus," she revealed with an uncertain smile. "I know this is not my husband's."

Shocked, he blurted out, "What? How is this possible?"

"Need I draw you a picture?" she replied sarcastically. "I agree, we need to end this. What we have can no longer continue. I will tell my husband it is his child; he will raise it as his own. Good luck with your future Perry. I sincerely hope America can offer you a better life than Treadwell has given you."

In his moment of sadness, Perry spoke, "My child will never know of me?"

"It is the way it has to be," she stared at him regrettably. "So much is at stake. I used you to continue the longevity of the Vision People. So much depends on what happens from here. You're a Visionary, Perry, someone who has the ability to change the future. Vampire Slayers were once rare; today they roam the world in droves. Now you are that rarity, once in a generation crap."

Perry picked up his carry-on luggage, "Go to hell!" He turned and walked away before halting to say his final words. "You're the worst bitch I have ever met."

"There are far worse bitches in this world, Vampire," she growled behind a humble smile. She watched him disappear through the International Departure gate.

~*~

*T*hree months passed, Perry had never returned to Treadwell.

Noah was displeased, and annoyed, his only ally had deserted him while his eldest brother remained in town, merely mortal because of his disliking of being a witch and the responsibilities it brought.

Settling into his life in the United States, Perry had forgotten about the woman, but struggled to put it out of his mind that he had fathered a child.

After another three months passed, and a new year began in Time Square with the dropping of the ball, Perry dabbled in homosexuality. He began a relationship with a French-Canadian male model named Sawyer Ashtoreth who hailed from the walled city of Quebec, Canada. After six months of his same-sex adventure, he returned to heterosexual relationships and began dating a woman.

Finally returning to Treadwell the following year, Perry walked through the airport with his luggage in toe. He wore jeans, brown boots, dress shirt, and a jacket.

Elevating his hand, he turned on his phone to see the time – 8.13pm was clear in bold text with a serene picture background. Suddenly, an in-coming call appeared on the screen as it rang, displaying a picture of his older brother Noah.

"Hello?" he said, placing the phone to his ear. "Noah, how are..." His brother on the other end cut him off mid-question. "Yes, I just cleared customs. I'm about to get into a taxi." He became silent again as he listened. "Okay. Okay. Calm down. I'll be there shortly, don't do anything stupid."

Immediately, he hung up.

He hurried through the airport and passed through the entry way as the automatic doors opened for him. Outside in the rain, he found the taxi rank empty. Frustrated, he grumbled to himself, raked his fingers through his hair and looked about. Noticing there were mortals in his immediate area, Perry found cover behind a concrete pillar.

"Take me to Noah," he said under his breath, "Teleportato," he commanded.

With his hand upon his luggage, he was transported to his brother's location in a pulse of energy.

Manifesting in another pulse of energy, Perry found himself in a dank and poorly lit cave. Stepping out from behind the rock, he was almost struck by a glimmering fireball as it shot through the air and exploded against the wall.

"Jesus," he gasped

In the middle of an open area, Noah Pogue ducked, weaved, levitated, and kicked a fast-moving opponent. Grumbling to himself as he watched his brother battle, Perry assumed his vampire visage and used his Accelerated Movement ability to move even faster.

Noah was flipped upside down and landed on his back with a thud. Perry terminated the altercation with the fast-moving individual suspended from the ground, his hand around its throat. He looked down at his brother who groaned.

"You rang?" Perry asked sarcastically. Turning his head, he looked back at the demon. "Quick little thing, aren't you?"

The demon's torso and legs flailed about in a speedy, blurred motion as it attempted to get free.

"Unfortunately for you, I am faster." Perry twisted his hand, and used his enhanced vampire strength to break the demon's neck.

The demon's body hung limp in his grip before disintegrating in a shimmer of flames.

"You were hunting a Velocius?" He queried his brother while retaining his vampire visage. "What on earth for?" Without warning, he was struck by something hard which sent him soaring across the cave and crashing into the wall.

The Pogue Book of Shadows depicts: Velocius, meaning faster in Latin, are a runt breed of demon who hunt and feed on Ogres. They stand at a height of four feet seven inches and have an emaciated figure. They can move fast often going unseen. If you wish to contend with these wicked things, use a blinding potion or make sure you have the power to stop time in order to stop them in their tracks.

Noah coughed, from where he lay on the ground, "Ogre!"

~*~

*R*eturning home to Noah's house, Perry stood in front of the roaring fire. The lounge room had a stone fireplace which looked like something you would find in a Canadian lodge, walls painted beige and comfortable, modern - for the time - leather lounge.

"You could have told me you were in Ogre Cave," Perry grumbled aloud. "The bast..." He quickly refrained from swearing when he saw his five-year-old nephew, Graeme, walk past the door. "The bugger had a wicked punch." He called out to the boy, "Hey, Graeme!"

Graeme Penthal smiled back at his uncle as he climbed the staircase dressed in his pajamas. In one hand, he clutched his favorite bear which head butted every step on the way up, in his other he carried a glass of warm milk.

"Oh," said a woman with delight. "You're home."

Connemara descended the staircase. Her long black hair floated in the air behind her as she rushed across the hallway and into the lounge room.

"I've missed you," she smiled upon approach. She hugged him and gave him a kiss on the lips.

Entering the room with two bottles of beer in his hands, Noah extended his arm and handed his brother a cold beverage. Connemara turned to face her husband and smiled at the two.

"Kathryn," Connemara called for her teenage sister to step forward. "Perry, I don't think you have met my youngest sister?"

A young, blonde haired woman, no older than nineteen, entered the room. "Kathryn, this is Noah's youngest brother."

Kathryn shook Perry's hand and they exchanged a smile.

Chapter Five

THE BUTCHART GARDEN OF GAIA

"In the garden of Butchart," Paimon cast a summoning spell.

"I call to the Goddess, Mother of Earth, unyielding in your power and captivating in your grace, your presence we embrace."

Immediately the snow began to glow, reality distorted, and finally a woman with a brilliant aura appeared. She was dressed in winter attire; suede boots, leggings, a woollen poncho and her long blonde hair was tied up in curls.

Accompanying her, sitting on a white leather high back chair with her legs crossed in a sophisticated manner, beneath a levitating white chandelier, was her daughter Rhea; Goddess of Fertility, Motherhood and the Mountain Wilds. Beside the chair, leaning on it with one muscle-defined arm, stood Pan, another god of nature. His torso and arms were nicely developed and defined while the lower half of his body represented a fawn's hindquarters, legs. He had the horns of a goat. In some variations of mythology, he is referred to as a satyr.

To the Mother's right, and a little behind; with his arms folded and dressed in a suit and a scarf; was the aloof male god, Dionysus.

Gaia stared at Paimon with a humble expression, but the unseen wrath behind it would tear trees from forests, and open fissures in the ground. She asked, "what urgencies bring you to our garden at this ungodly hour?"

Bermuda murmured softly, "tell me about it, it's fricken cold!"

Gaia shot her a harsh glare, and immediately intimidated the young witch.

"You brought witches?" She studied the three sisters curiously. "Pogue Witches at that." Her hard face softened as if recalling a love affair. "Pray tell, Bermuda Pogue. Did you come all this way from Treadwell?"

Bermuda remained silent as she stared curiously at the deity.

Gaia responded, "my mortal name, alias, if you will, is Cynthea Houston. Surely you know the need for discretion in a world unable to comprehend what is beyond its reasoning. We have, and exercise, mortal names so we may go unnoticed."

"You're Gaia," Isadora smirked with disbelief, "You're her, Lights Vision of..."

Gaia smiled. "Colonel William Lightfoot. A great man. An honour just to know him." She unphased by the chilly wind and snow. "My roots are deep in Treadwell. But that Leviathan, that Hellmouth, deters me, deters us." Gaia gestured toward her fellow earth deities. "Dionysus, my daughter Rhea and Pan. We choose to reside here, in the Butchart Gardens."

Dionysus spoke in a deep and imposing voice, "What is it you want, Paimon?"

The ancient demon, and the three Pogue sisters peered past the deity before them, and they listened to the proud man standing beyond her in a glow of moonlight.

"My allegiance is to evil, I'm a demon," Paimon spoke arrogantly.

Rhea snarled, "and, we are gods, would you rather we smite you?"

Paimon continued, "I helped Rafaela pull a demon from the Dream World to here, the Real World." Unhappy with the revelations, Gaia initiated a deafening crack of thunder accompanied by a flash of lightning. "She possessed a Babylon Crystal, what was I to do?"

Rhea remarked nastily, "the lengths some demons go to in order to cover their own asses. Perhaps the Hell Goddess should have vanquished you with the crystal as soon as she achieved what she wanted!"

Andromeda interjected. "I stole the crystal from her."

Rhea nodded her head, and smirked at the ironic situation Paimon had found himself in.

"We are using the crystal as leverage to gain access to the Dream World, with the aid of his inter-dimensional powers," Andromeda finished.

"With power such as that, Paimon, you ought to be a god." Pan laughed. "Did you tell them how the crystal weakens your power? And, how you're only complying, because you know if you get your hands on the crystal, you can destroy it and resume your full level of power."

Bermuda growled, "the moron told us he would need the help of Garden Magic to assist him in opening a portal to the Dream World. We have to go there to rescue some family members."

"He thinks we're in debt to him." Sarcasm oozed from Rhea's voice. "Why, is beyond even us," she lied. "We do not show servitude to anything evil."

~*~

*S*ome sixty years ago, Rhea, daughter of the goddess Gaia, had

intervened in an escalating situation between the demon, Asmodeus, and magical creatures of the Garden Magic realm.

Running through the city streets of Victoria, Vancouver Island, British Columbia; demon, Asmodeus fled with his lover, Paimon. They had massacred a group of Wood Nymphs and their Satyr, in the water fountain in front of the British Columbia Parliament Buildings on Superior Street. They had captured the Satyr and used him to sing his flute to lure the beautiful women to their deaths in the mortal world.

Reaching the half-way point of the Johnson Street Bridge, Rhea manifested in a lightning strike, bringing Asmodeus and Paimon to halt. In retaliation, both demons conjured balls of fire into their hands and attacked the deity.

"From above, upon ground, last forever, until he's slain, turn Paimon's lover into ice." Casting her spell to the sky, she conjured up snow.

The Port Angeles of Victoria was, for a moment, turned to ice.

Crying out in agony, Asmodeus turned away attempted to flee from the powerful deity. But, the cost of his evil act against creatures of nature, was to be turned into a statue of solid ice.

"What have you done?" Paimon roared in rage.

Rhea faced him with a smug expression. "As long as you live, he will remain in ice. Your possession, the Babylon Crystal, will forever be your weakness, not your empowerment."

In a rumble of thunder, and flash of lightning, Rhea vanished and the Port Angeles was released from her spell. Beside him on the bridge, his lover, Asmodeus, was encased in solid ice.

~*~

Rhea smirked arrogantly as she and Paimon made eye contact.

"I guess everything at the end of the day, is good for business. Right, Paimon?"

Closing his eyes for a moment, he heard her voice in his mind. "No matter how many good witches you assist, I will never unfreeze your lover, Asmodeus. You cannot kill good creatures and expect no ramifications, Demon. Not in our jurisdiction."

Opening his eyes, and in a fit of rage, Paimon moved his arm from his side, conjured a ball of fire and attempted to throw it at Gaia.

"STAY OUT OF MY HEAD," he roared.

Protecting herself, Gaia extended her arm and faced the palm of her hand at the demon.

"BANDIRE!"

Her voice bellowed into the silence of the night, and she banished him from the Butchart Gardens. His arms extended to his sides, his fiery attack was extinguished, and his back arched. Paimon's body then dispersed into molecules which were sucked into one another before vanishing in a speck of light.

Isadora's jaw dropped. "Uh, excuse me, we kind of needed him to...get to the Dream World." She glanced at her sisters before returning her focus to Gaia. "Didn't we?"

Gaia stepped forward. "He was using you, manipulating you. You promised him the crystal if he brought you here. But, he knew we'd never assist him. A allowing him to open a portal to the Dream World, would enable him to pull Mangiare Demons into this world. This is something I would never permit, so forgive me for banishing him. He is a risk I wish not to entertain."

Bermuda spoke, "but, demons snarl and they return, it's what they do."

"We're well aware," Gaia replied. "You three girls are seasoned witches, but not seasoned enough to gauge the power of manipulation. Paimon did not divulge that only your subconscious enters the Dream World, not your physical body."

Andromeda realized the truth and fury reddened her face, "Oh, that sneaky bast..." She immediately stopped herself from swearing in front of a deity. "Sneaky batman. He would have used the opportunity to steal the crystal and regain his powers."

Isadora raised her eyebrow, "Batman?"

Dionysus spoke from the back, "Only a god can grant you a physical form in an obscure realm like the Dream World. It's a world that mirrors this one. It will appear the same in every fact, but is unstable enough to continuously change what you see with the slightest thought." He recalled an important detail. "It is home to the aboriginal races, First Nations, Native Americans and the Australian Dream Time People."

"Don't forget The Morrígan," Rhea interrupted,

Dionysus thought for a moment, "Oh, and an Old One."

Gaia approached and placed her hand over each of the witch's hearts. "I grant you this, a solid form, in every realm you venture to." She then recited a rhyme. "When you feel the Kindred call, no act of love will ever be small!"

With a sway of her arm and flick of her wrist, Gaia transported the three sister witches to the Dream World.

"Safe travels," she murmured to herself.

Gaia, Rhea, Pan, and Dionysus, vanished in flashes of light, returning to their hidden sanctuary within the Butchart Gardens. Decorated by delicate lights, the gardens returned to a winter wonderland.

~*~

Under the street lights of the parking lot of the Butchart Gardens, before the front gates and welcome board; a swarm of black buzzing molecules gathered. Forming to one black mass, it glowed a bold red. Crying out in agony, Paimon manifested. His arms jerked and flailed before calming by his sides.

"Ugh," he groaned uncomfortably and ran his fingers through his salt and pepper hair. "I hate gods." Furious his ploy had failed, he allowed his demon side to almost manifest. His eyes glowed red and horns emerged out of his head. "Rhea, you will pay for..."

"Impressive," interrupted a woman's voice.

Paimon immediately returned to his human visage and acknowledged a sumptuous woman standing across from him. He took a moment to study her - long dark hair, she wore a black knitted dress, grey leggings, black boots and waist length emerald coloured cape.

"Who are you?" he growled. Studying her, he came to realize they had met once before. "I know you. I've seen you before." Concentration appeared in his face as he read her glittering aura. "Connemara Preston."

She smiled. "Cornacchia Monarch, to you, small fry." Elevating her hand, she flicked her fingers. "Julyanne," she called out, making the High Priestess of British Columbia visible to Paimon. "Trap him."

A stunned Paimon was unable to move. His path blocked by a fast-moving blur of gray cicling him, and placed five white crystals on the ground around him. Reappearing at Connemara Preston's side, she had revealed her power of Sonic Speed. An advanced version of the Accelerated Speed.

"What?" Paimon roared. When he attempted to step forward, the magical trap reacted. It admitted flashes, and sparks of light. "What is this?" He studied the two women. "A demon working with a good, High Priestess. This is barbaric. Wait until Rafaela hears about your espionage."

"It's Connemara Penthal, thank you." Reaching into her pocke,t she threw his Babylon Crystal into the air in front of her. "You tried to deceive three witches tonight. And this," using magic she froze the crystal in midair. "This restores the power Rhea took from you. But, I have a way around that."

Paimon smiled, his ploy to get his rightful power back was only moments away.

Connemara cast a vanquishing spell on the crystal. "Upon you, I do impart. Vanquish this demon." The crystal glowed red. Paimon realized what she was doing when intense heat filled every part of his body. "Spare," Paimon cried out in agony. "No part!"

In a scream of agony, Paimon's body exploded into tiny molecules with a shimmer of flames in the centre claiming the demon essence at his core. Releasing her magic from the crystal, she witnessed it disintegrate into dust.

"My dear," spoke the mature woman beside her in a cold voice. "Now I have assisted you in the vanquishing of your demon, we must discuss the conniving issue of those three witches who bypassed the agreement and regulations of my jurisdiction. I did not grant them passage, or use of their magic here in British Columbia. They used talismans to harness their magic."

"I respect and understand your position Julyanne. However, I too, have a predicament. I vanquished the original Cornacchia Monarch, and assumed her identity in order to protect certain members of the Pogue Family."

Julyanne spoke cautiously, "because of the Illusory you have in place. I understand and fully comprehend your position. But, my policy stands firm Ms. Penthal. All good witches must, like Border Security for mortals when entering a foreign country, check-in. I cannot tolerate unmonitored individuals hiding, or unleashing unspeakable acts. When I am aware, I am able to execute the right protocols, and not have the Canadian Prime Minister or Police Commissioner raking me over the coals."

"My apologies," Connemara accepted the responsibility like the noble woman she was. "I will see to it, myself, personally."

Julyanne replied, "it is settled. I must be going; I am to return to Ladysmith." Her aura burned gold, her body teleported away and her outline finally vanished too.

~*~

Connemara shrieked when she was abruptly projected backwards onto the ground. Lifting her head, she sat up, and watched a modest man walk out of the dark at the edge of the parking lot. His walk was distinct with over-inflated confidence, he was unshaven with stubble about his jaw-line, and his greasy black hair was styled back.

His body flickered like an old television before disappearing, and then reappearing again, directly in front of the beautiful enchantress.

"Who are you?" She demanded to know.

Grabbing her by the collar, he elevated her from the ground. "I am Sabar, the Sabarticar Demon. I am a hunter of secrets and desires, Rafaela sent me on a mission. I've been searching for you, fraud. I know all about your dirty secrets, witch."

Connemara shrieked when Sabar was attacked by a foreign object, knocking him aside, and she was thrown backwards onto the ground again. Looking up, she caught a glimpse of a beautiful woman with long red hair.

"Rubella, the Siren?"

The red-haired woman replied, "go, Connemara. It's not safe. I can handle him." She anticipated the demon's approaching attack, spun around and projected bolts of iridescent red energy at him. Extending her arm toward the witch, Rubella cast a spell on her. "To a place, she ought to be, I send you home, to the Siren Sorority."

Sabar roared. "Nooo, the Witch is Mine!"

Connemara felt a glowing light descend over her body as she was teleported away, after witnessing the beautiful red-haired Siren being knocked out of view by a black figure.

~*~

Gasping for air, a terrified Connemara Penthal reappeared in a white leather, high back chair in the drawing room of a picturesque manor. Light shone through the ceiling to floor windows. She stood from the chair, confused, disoriented.

"Connemara Penthal," a voice said from behind her.

Spinning around, she was greeted by a group of stylish women, each with different colored hair.

"Welcome to the Siren Sorority Witness Protection. My name is Lana Pratt, the leader."

THE FACELESS MAN

*T*here came the sound of the ocean washing against the gravel shore of Gowland Point, Pender Island, Canada. Although winter in Canada, perfect warm sunshine shone down on the two men as they lay side-by-side watching one another die.

Perry Pogue stretched his arm out and rested his hand in Noah's.

"I'm," he fumbled through his words emotionally. "I'm so sorry, I hurt you."

The wind picked up suddenly, emitting a yell. Perry was pulled away and thrown across the beach by Kamenwati's Telekinesis. Resting on his back for a moment he sighed, thinking the worst was over. He was wrong. He was electrocuted by her power of Black Lightning, and elevated from the ground as he cried out in agony.

"How does it feel?"

Kamenwati approached with her arms extended, hands facing upwards; black electricity flashed, and flicked off, in various directions. Her dark smile radiated against her impeccable complexion.

Perry continued crying out in agony as he levitated six feet off the ground.

She continued to taunt him, "how does it feel to watch your brother die right in front of you?" Noah lay on the ground, his head tilted to the side, his still eyes vacant of all life. "Knowing you were the cause of his death!"

Perry continued to cry out in agony. Closing his eyes, visions of the past via the Recognition branch of his main Sensazione power invaded his thoughts. He saw his mother, his father - Gregory Fox, handsome and manly with a blazing golden aura only a Sentinel possessed. Aaron appeared next, and turned his back on his younger brother. Perry remembered the day his eldest brother had relinquished his magic to live out a mortal life. He held a child in his arms. Finally, he saw his brother, Noah, lying dead beside him on the beach.

Opening his eyes, he focused his strength by letting out an ear-splitting roar. The pain of the excruciating attack quickly diminished, and his face morphed as he assumed his vampire visage. He released a telekinetic pulse which released his body from the black electricity and used his vampire powers to move with an accelerated speed.

"Hear now, the witches' rhyme." A synchronization of voices chanted a spell as they manifested on the wind, "Cross the skies."

Kamenwati deactivated her power. "Bring it on Filipino witches." Extending her arm in front of her, her hair blew back and created a barrier. "I've got what I need."

"No place to hide," the voices continued to cast their spell. "Even in the mind, devil kind, we break your bind; release the witch to our place and time."

In a blinding flash of light, a fast-moving Perry vanished. Glancing toward the beach, a dumbfounded Kamenwati acknowledged Noah's disappearance also.

Aryan spoke from behind her, "unfortunately you're the one who is going to pay the price."

Paimon's summoning spell moved on the wind. "Across the bridge, the dimension is passed, bring down the veil, let my power surpass. I call to thee, Kamenwati, your attendance belongs with me."

Kamenwati turned, and the Filipino Witch placed her hand on the demon's forehead. She let out an agonizing scream before exploding into black smoke. The smoke was drawn together at the centre, and disappeared in a flicker of light.

"Huh?" a dumbfounded, fight ready Aryan queried.

~*~

The path was filled with blinding light and the distinct sound of eighties music could be heard. *Olivia Newton-John's* song '*Xanadu*' was being performed. Gasping as they entered into the new reality of the Dream World, Isadora, Bermuda, and Andromeda found themselves in the middle of a disco dance floor in a nightclub.

Bermuda noted the dancing individuals. "Oh god, we're in eighties hell."

Isadora pointed, "they have great voices." Bermuda and Andromeda turned toward the stage where their sister had pointed. Three women, using their Siren abilities performed the song. Isadora queried, "Are they for real? People actually dream of singing songs?"

"This is a world made up of the sub-conscious," Bermuda reminded.

Isadora agreed.

"This way, let's hope it's our way out." Weaving through the bodies on the crowded dance floor, Andromeda led her sisters to a door at the rear of the dark, and cigarette smoke filled, club.

"I wonder if people will start dancing on roller blades," Isadora swung her hips in time to the song. "I'm sorry," she apologized when Bermuda pierced her with a sour look.

Andromeda used her power of Molecular Combustion to blast the lock on the door, and throw it open. Behind them, unseen, the three women performing on stage glared with hostility before leaping onto the crowded dance floor. They assumed a black smoke form, and silently weaved amongst the mortals toward the three unsuspecting witches.

Passing through the doorway, the three sisters emerged into the large hallway of a house with polished timber floorboards and white painted walls. Ahead of them, at the opposite end was a large, farm style front door which opened out to a yard bathed in warm daylight.

"Now, where the hell are we?" Isadora asked as the three walked along. She glanced to her side, and noted the painting on the wall. "I've seen this somewhere before." An elusive truth was staring her right in the face.

Andromeda paused, looked around at the walls, floor and up at the ceiling.

"Why does this house feel so familiar?" Bermuda asked no-one in particular.

Andromeda spoke cautiously, "be careful, this dimension is truth. It's a world of total sub-conscious, where all lies fail."

"Oh, you're home," a delighted woman squealed.

A startled Bermuda slid to a stop, her eyes open wide.

Hearing the voice, Isadora turned and Andromeda stiffened.

To their right, a woman descended the staircase to their right. Long black hair floated behind her as she rushed across the hallway, and disappeared into a lounge room to the left.

"What the hell?" Bermuda sputtered.

Isadora stood at Andromeda's side, "Who the hell was that?"

Andromeda replied hesitantly, "I have no fricken idea."

The two sisters hurried up the hallway to Bermuda and stood. Three sets of eyes stared at the doorway the woman had disappeared through.

"You go first." Andromeda nudged her twin in the back.

Bermuda glared at her. "Why me?"

Isadora murmured, "Because we're too pretty to die, it might be a trap."

Andromeda replied and shoved Bermuda in the back. "What she said, now go."

"We go together!" Bermuda hissed.

Andromeda replied in a huff, "Fine."

Together, the three sisters moved toward the door cautiously and stopped. Peering in, they observed a male, kissing the woman passionately. Isadora's attention was drawn by a noise, and she noticed the door they had come through into the house had closed by itself. Glancing upward toward the ceiling, she caught a glimpse of black smoke before it disappeared. She tapped Andromeda on the shoulder,

"Err, guys, I don't think we're..."

Andromeda warned her sister, "be careful Bermuda."

Intrigued, Isadora turned her attention back to the unfolding passion in the lounge room before them.

Sneaking into the occupied room, it quickly became apparent to Bermuda Pogue, neither she, nor the man and woman, seemed aware of the presence of one another. She informed her sisters,

"I think what we are seeing, is a vision of the past, or something relative to it. It's nothing we can affect because it's someone else's sub-conscious."

Andromeda spoke from her position in the doorway, "be careful. Even if it's someone else's sub-conscious, it's a hidden truth. Whoever sees it, will be affected by it. Like, once you see something, you cannot unsee it."

Isadora mused, "a domino effect?"

"Pretty much," Andromeda replied.

Standing behind the woman, Bermuda waited for the moment when the male's face would be revealed. The result was what her sister had warned about, seeing something she wish she had not. She felt the blood drain from her face and knew she must be left her as white as a ghost, an unnerving feeling danced in the pit of her stomach. She saw something which validated a lot for her, and her, life.

Andromeda, noting how pale her sister had become, hurried into the room. "Are you okay? What is...it?" Her eyebrows raised, and a look of confusion crossed her face. "He has no face. How strange."

Isadora hurried into the room to see for herself this peculiar thing which had left one of her sisters startled, and the other perplexed.

She agreed with Andromeda. "His face is blank. No eyes, no mouth, nothing. Perhaps his identity is not ours to know."

Now confused, Bermuda questioned her sisters. "You're telling me you cannot see his face? I see it as plain as day. He has a nose, green eyes, eyebrows, lips and stubble."

"Do you know him?" Isadora asked.

Bermuda hesitated before lying. "No. No, I don't."

The couple in front of them suddenly, without warning, vanished. In the doorway three enchanting women stood. Dressed in black, it was obvious what their nature was.

The woman in the middle warned. "You should not have come here, it's not safe for those who do not know the way around."

Isadora remembered, "They were the singers in the club..."

The woman on the left cut her off. "We are Mangiare."

Andromeda grumbled with irritation, "I should have known there would be demons here. They are Dream Devourers."

"Excuse me, there are demons, here?" Isadora asked, puzzled.

Her sister nodded.

"In the Dream World?" Isadora absorbed the idea in its entirety. "Makes sense I guess. Nightmares, demons; they're all tarred with the same brush really."

Retaliating, the Mangiare in the centre stretched her arms forward and projected bolts of black lightning at the three sisters.

Shrieking, Isadora acted on instinct and extended her arm, manipulated energy around herself, and her siblings, and created a barrier which kept the black magic at arm's length, but didn't deflect it.

The Mangiare on the left spoke confidently. "We're immune to the powers of witches, you have no strength against us."

Andromeda cast a spell. "To every breath, your heart does quicken. Starved you are, the air does thicken."

The Mangiare on the right stepped forward, and the air around her warped brilliantly.

Panicked, she beckoned her leader by name, "Kati."

Kati, the Mangiare in the centre, lowered her arms and deactivated her black lightning power when she realized; in the Dream World, a witch's magic did have an effect on them.

Insulted, the demon on the left, in a gleam of red, conjured a knife into her hand and threw it at Bermuda.

Manoeuvring her arm through the air, Bermuda used her power of Deflection to repel the knife from her and her sisters. Impaled in the head, the demon trapped in distorted air, let out a piercing scream and was vanquished in a shimmer of flames.

Screaming in a fit of fury, the Mangiare on the left of Kati leapt into the air and assumed her black smoke form. Surging across the distance to the three Pogue witches, she was halted when Andromeda extended her arm.

"Air thicken, now disfigured, give her back her human figure."

Instantly the demon resumed her human form and stared at the witch before her.

Andromeda spoke arrogantly, "this is the Dream World, moron. Your immunity to witches is now diminished, it only exists in the mortal world to prevent people like us from vanquishing your ugly ass."

The still demon, trapped in thick, unmoving air in front of the three sisters squawked.

"Kati!" Her eyes snapped to the left as she glanced over her shoulders. She trembled at the idea of being vanquished and showed a moment of weakness. "Tell them where the Visionary is, I don't want to die."

Kati, standing in the doorway, displayed a very cold and uncaring demeanour. "Shut up! Do not utter another word you feeble idiot, or I will dispose of you myself."

Startled by the bold attitude, Isadora raised an eyebrow.

The still demon spoke with regard toward Bermuda which was an uncommon gesture amongst Nightmare Soldiers, "you saw his face, you know who he is. It means you, are also a Visionary. You're destined to change the course of the– argh!!" Screaming in agony she was vanquished in a shimmering flame.

Kati stepped into the room, with a brisk swing of her arm and driven with arrogance, she threw Isadora to the side with telekinesis and disrupted her power of Energy Manipulation.

"This is my world, you possess nowhere near the amount of power I do, witch." Kati grinned, her eyes glowed silver and her aura burned black.

Andromeda fired her power of Molecular Combustion, creating a blast of flickering flames against Kati's body.

The demon smirked confidently, "You call that, power? I have heard of your coming, the promising power of the Pogue Witches. But so far, all I have seen," reaching both arms out in front of her, she projected bolts of black lightning at the twin sister witches. "IS WEAKNESS!"

Raising her arm, and turning the palm of her hand to the oncoming attack, Andromeda used her own power of Energy Manipulation to create a barrier. Away to the side, lying on her side, Isadora raised her head. Brushing her hair away from her face, she reached into her pocket, pulled out a pendant which bore the symbol of the goddess, Venus, and threw it at the demon. It attached itself to Kati's clothes.

Isadora cast her vanquishing spell and the pendant began to glow. "I call to thee, I am her servant and she is my queen. Light of Venus, come aid me. Vanquish this evil entity."

Kati deactivated her power for a moment and chuckled. "Really? is that all you've got?"

Then, blasting down through the ceiling, leaving a gaping hole in its wake, a brilliant beam of light eclipsed Kati. Letting out a scream of agony, her body exploded into a fireball which disappeared along with the light.

Bermuda and Andromeda glanced at their sister; watching as she scrambled back onto her feet.

Bermuda spoke, "how..." she corrected herself, "no, where the hell do we go from here? If this world is made up of the sub-conscious, chances are a single thought good or bad could have dangerous effects within this uncharted world."

"I don't care. All I fricken know, is, we need to get out of here." Isadora grumbled. "Now. We don't have time for this crap. Rafaela has Kamenwati, so where the hell does that leave us?"

Shrieking, she dropped back to the floor when fast moving arrows smashed through the windows from the outside and impaled furniture and walls.

Bermuda had a look of terror as she hid behind the sofa.

"You had to fricken ask?" she growled at Isadora.

Ripping an arrow from the wall, Andromeda made a revelation, "it seems we may have given ourselves away and pissed off some First Nations."

Isadora asked nervously, "where do we go, what do we do? I'm not sure I want to have a man versus wild encounter– ah!" She shrieked when another arrow flew in through the window. She used her magic to halt the projectile in the air at an arm's distance from her.

Chapter Seven

VISIONARY PART SIX

"Let's go upstairs," Andromeda insisted as she began to devise a plan. "If this is a sub-conscious world, then we ought to be able to summon the sub-conscious version of our book of shadows to wherever we are. And, if I remember correctly, this place has an attic too."

Bermuda queried, "Now you're speaking as though you know this place?"

"I remember this place, now. This is Grandma's holiday house on Gabriola Island," Andromeda said.

"Why would you have a holiday house in the Hamptons, when you could have one in Canada?" Isadora retorted as she, and Bermuda both made odd unknowing facial gestures.

There was a moment of silence, the arrows being fired into the house by First Nations had ceased.

"It's worth a shot," Bermuda encouraged. "What was that riddle Gaia said about being kindred?"

Andromeda replied with bittersweet sarcasm, "who cares at the moment? Clearly our priorities should be elsewhere, sister. Or, haven't you noticed we're being fired upon by Pocahontas?"

Andromeda and her sisters rose from their crouching positions and quickly made their move across the room while there was a break in the hostilities. Letting out a sudden shriek, Isadora was narrowly missed as an arrow impaled the wooden door frame.

If she had been a few seconds earlier, she would have been impaled instead.

From the staircase across the hallway, Andromeda summoned her sister, "Indy move your bloody arse or you will become a witch-kebab."

Turning slightly, Isadora extended her arm and curled her fingers at the pendant she had used to vanquish Kati that lay on the floor.

"Venite ad me, (Come to me)" she spoke in Latin,

Telekinetically, it moved from the ground and into her hand.

~*~

Outside, in the beautiful sunshine, the three storey, white timber and sandstone manor, partly covered in ivy, was hemmed in by the beautiful evergreen Canadian forest.

Emerging from the shadows of the tree trunks, six grizzly bears rose onto their hind legs and shapeshifted into humans – four men and two women. They wore nothing more than pieces of brown leather to cover their genital area and breasts. They were the superior clan of the First Nations who inhabited the realm. The Omega, led by Chief Alo.

"FIRE!" Chief Alo, a tall, masculine male with knee high boots made of fur, and leather straps around his right hand and metal talons, ordered his kin. "KILL THE WITCHES!"

Arching their bows, and readying their javelins, the six clan members fired their arrows and threw their weapons at the manor. Plummeting down from the sunny sky, a brilliant orb of heavenly light touched the ground. A beautiful woman with red hair pulled back in a ponytail, and dressed in roman warrior attire, appeared.

Swiftly extending her arm, she projected wondrous light, turning the arrows, and javelins to dust.

"You have no right to attack those who wish not to engage you," she growled at the natives. "I am Diana, Goddess of the Hunt and I am ordering you to let the witches be. They are not harming you, or disfiguring your realm. You are good hospitable people, what is wrong with you?"

Alo replied in his deep voice, "we do not like witches, good or evil. There was once a time when we had an allegiance, but that was before they assimilated into white man's way of living and abandoned ours."

Diana had successfully created a diversion so her partner and gay witch, Julyanne, High Priestess of British Columbia, could enter the manor to help the three Pogue sisters escape and get to where they were supposed to be.

Where the closed front doors to the manor should have been, a glowing blue portal manifested. Julyanne stepped through into the lobby before closing the portal behind her.

"Where are they?" she queried to the empty house.

Manifesting into existence, the ghost of Carmen Penthal appeared to her left. "They are upstairs. Those Neanderthals nearly killed them, Julyanne." Together they approached the staircase to the right, and ventured upwards.

Julyanne appeared to be as displeased. "I am aware, but they were never supposed to come here, to this part of the Dream World. They were meant to go straight to Perry and Noah's location."

"I don't think Gaia would have sent them here deliberately." A cautious Carmen did her best to sound confident in the goodness of the earth deity. "Gaia must have read their auras instead of reading their thoughts. Only their auras would have sent them here."

Julyanne replied with new found knowledge, "there is a lot more to this sticky situation, which I am sure you are aware of, considering you're the deceased sister of both Connemara and Kathryn Penthal."

Carmen smiled at the correlation.

"It was within recent hours, I was made aware your sister has placed an Illusory around the Pogue family to protect them from an evil which seeks resurrection."

Carmen spoke as they reached the hallway of the second storey. "My sister is not dark minded or evil spirited, Julyanne. Connor, I believe would have only done it out of obligation to protect the family she married into. She is one of the Government Supernatural Bureau's finest and one of Maria's most powerful witches. However, to shroud someone's mind from knowing the truth of where they come from, is unfair. It's a dark secret to keep from a lot of people, but if it is being executed for the sake of their own safety..." She lost the direction of her argument as they approached a narrow staircase leading up to the attic.

"I don't like lies. This realm is notorious for revealing secrets and Bermuda saw the face of the man downstairs who kisses your sister. You know what that means, and what repercussions it's going to have."

Entering the attic of the house, Julyanne stood in the doorway, while Carmen remained invisible. The door swung back, and slammed against the wall, causing Isadora and Bermuda to shriek and jump in fright.

"Julyanne," Andromeda whispered.

Isadora's eyes widened awkwardly, "oh crap, she's going to crucify us."

Julyanne replied calmly. "Ladies, you should not be here. This house is not a sanctuary; you've already found that out the hard way."

Bermuda asked, "who is the woman beside you?"

Isadora and Andromeda gazed at their sister with confusion. They could only see Julyanne in the doorway. Because Bermuda possessed the power of Sensazione, the Mediumship branch of the power allowed her to see ghosts.

"There is a ghost beside me." Julyanne spoke knowingly, revealing that she too, possessed the same power as the Pogue Witch. "Carmen occupies this house, but enough small talk and comparing powers, Bermuda Pogue, you need to leave."

Carmen spoke to Bermuda, "the natives outside this house don't like witches. They are not evil, but they will kill you where you stand should you linger here any longer."

"I know you, but where have I met you?" Bermuda asked Carmen.

Julyanne murmured to the deceased witch beside her, "Don't utter a word. Remember the flaws of this realm, you risk doing a lot of damage if you tell her the truth."

Carmen remained silent.

"The Deity, Gaia sent you here by mistake. I can create a portal so you can get to where you are supposed to be. Diana, is outside creating a diversion, so you may leave without engaging the natives," Julyanne advised the three sisters.

Andromeda replied, "uh, okay. Thank you. We were going to summon the spirit version of our Book of Shadows here to find a spell to send us to our uncles. But, if you are able to create a portal, it would very much appreciated."

Showing noticeable discomfort, Bermuda rubbed firmly into the left side of her chest as a niggling pain returned. Turning her head slightly, she closed her eyes and murmured as the discomfort increased.

Julyanne frowned with concern, "are you okay, Bermuda?"

"I'm okay. I have a niggling pain in my heart, like something is trying to warn me..." she winced again. Gasping, she closed her eyes and had a premonition of Perry Pogue in his vampire visage. She groaned as she crumpled to the ground. "..I," she stuttered.

Isadora dropped to the floor beside her. "Bermuda, Oh my god. You're not okay."

Andromeda asked, "what did you see?"

Bermuda replied when the discomfort eased for a moment, "Perry, he was wearing his vampire face. Something is not right." She closed her eyes and when she opened them, she saw Perry, in his vampire visage, stood in the middle of the room. Bermuda stared at him. "why are you here?"

Turning to face where Bermuda was staring, Isadora and Andromeda saw only an empty area, where their sister saw something else.

Perry growled at her in an animalistic way before charging toward her. "I'm hungry, I want your blood. Let me feed on you, witch!"

Bermuda screamed and raised her arms to shield herself from him as he approached. He grabbed her by the arm, vanished into thin air, and she was teleported out of the house in a flash of golden light.

"Bermuda!" Andromeda shrieked in terror, before questioning Julyanne, "what just happened? Where did she go?"

A panicked Isadora shook, "what scared her like that?"

Entering further into the room, and closing the door behind her, Julyanne locked it to prevent the natives, outside on the lawn, from entering the attic, and attacking, should they gain entry to the house. Turning around she re-engaged the two remaining sisters.

She informed them of the ill-fated objectives this world upheld. "In this world, there are many flaws. Because this world is based entirely on the sub-conscious, and spirituality, the deceased are able to come and go as they please from your dreams."

Andromeda snapped, "get to the point."

Julyanne glared at her. "In this world, you rude little witch, there is a thing called the Whisper of the Kindred. Where your heart and soul, if you will, calls to someone you love who has been separated from you for a significant amount of time."

Isadora asked, "like mourning?"

"Exactly, but that is within reason," Julyanne replied politely. "Except, here, the person you miss may not be deceased, but in another part of the human world. The point is, when your sub-conscious is asleep, you will be drawn to one another. But, because you're here in full corporeal form, which goes against the law of this dimension, hence the term sub-conscious again, that call is going to feel like your heart is being torn out."

Andromeda spoke, "hmm, Whisper of the Kindred, Gaia mentioned something to us before she teleported us here - 'When you feel the Kindred call, no act of love will ever be small.' Is that what she was trying to tell us in a round-about way?"

Julyanne answered, "yes, now come here, and I will cast the spell to help you get to the same place as your sister."

Approaching the middle of the room, Isadora and Andromeda took one another's hands and then each took Julyanne's hands.

"Hear our words, feel our pain, we cast our call across this ancient plane, to seek a sister who is misplaced, aboriginal goddess Gnowee, take them to Bermuda Pogue's place."

Directly in the center of the three women, a spiral of twinkling light rose from the floor and a regal aboriginal woman manifested. She wore pieces of tribal clothing on her body and carried a staff in her left hand.

"Mote it be," she said with sympathy.

With her free hand, she waved at the two sisters, transporting them away in a quick flash of golden light. Just as quick as she had manifested, the goddess Gnowee was gone. Left absent in the attic, Julyanne stared at the large bay window, and then at the vast forest beyond.

Carmen stepped out from behind Julyanne. "Has it begun?"

Julyanne didn't make eye contact with the deceased witch. "As foretold, the vampire tormented by his dreams, will kill his brother, and the path for the beast's resurrection will be made. Light will become gray, and the balance will tilt toward evil." She folded her arms and concern showed in her face. "The Pogue Witches were once an unrivalled power, but their power is broken. Rafaela and her evil forces continue to escalate, and I'm not so sure that the remaining good of the world can stand against her."

Carmen sympathised, "if we have nothing, then we must have faith, High Priestess."

Julyanne spoke over her shoulder, "Something dark is coming, regardless of faith, my dear witch. For you are already deceased, you have no role to play in the scheme of things." she gazed toward the window again. "My faith is in these young witches. The next generation possess great power, and this coming darkness will want to take it for themselves. I am not entirely sure I favour your sister's ploy to cast an Illusory to hide them from their destiny."

Outside, standing as a diversion, Diana with a wave of her arm, and gesture of her hand, used her power of Molecular Dispersion to send the First Nations away; scattering their bodies into molecules and sent them adrift on the breeze.

~*~

On the beach of Gowlland Point, Pender Island, British Columbia, Canada, the waves crashed and then withdrew, repeating the process over and over. Waves broke over the rocks just meters into the water itself, the water spraying into the air. The sound of gulls could be heard overhead.

The beautiful Mongkukulam – Filipino term for witch – Aryan, stood on the sand with a cowering Bermuda behind her, and her arm extended toward two Mangiare Demons who stood opposed. Black lightning coiled off in various directions as Aryan upheld a glittering barrier which she was mentally conjuring with the daylight.

"The Visionary comes with us," one hissed loudly. "You die, Mongkukulam."

Aryan yelled back, "the witch stays with me."

Behind her, glows of golden light manifested as Isadora and Andromeda were transported to the location of their sister.

Isadora halted beside the Filipino witch, and immediately cast a vanquishing spell which was amplified by her Photokinesis power. "Light of day, shall not wane, combust you shall." The pitch of her voice rose, and echoed about the immediate area. "INTO FLAMES! INTO FLAMES!"

Shrieking in pain, the two Mangiare Demons were vanquished in glimmering flames which left thick, black scorch marks on the sand. Andromeda knelt down to her sister and comforted her.

Aryan turned to Isadora. "Who are you?" Then, acknowledging the witch's stunning indigo coloured eyes, she suddenly found herself overcome with excitement. "You're her, Isadora Pogue."

Isadora stood proudly. "She is me, Isadora Pogue."

"Aryan," she introduced herself.

Isadora looked her over. "You're a Mongkukulam, are you not?"

"Yes, Yes, I am," Aryan replied.

Andromeda interrupted as she comforted Bermuda. "We are searching for Prometheus Pogue, and his brother, Noah. Have you seen them?"

Aryan nodded. "Yes, I have! Kamenwati had Perry..."

Andromeda rose as Bermuda settled. "Kamenwati had Perry what? There is no cat to have your tongue, speak now witch, or I could spell you."

VISIONARY PART SEVEN

The wind blew through the tops of the trees along Stanley Point. Over on this side of Pender Island, the skies were grey and it rained in the Dream World. Thunder rumbled as the presence of evil clashed with good forces of the realm. The temperate evergreen rainforest hugged both sides of the road, making them feel narrow, and gloomy, under the wintery sky.

At the bend of Walden Road, where it met Susan Point Road, a golden spectacle appeared, and grew larger, before it disappeared. In its wake stood Isadora, Andromeda, Bermuda, and Aryan the Filipino witch. Raindrops washed over them as they scanned first to their right, the dead-end of Walden Road, and then ahead, up Susan Point Road.

Isadora asked, "Which way do we go?"

Andromeda turned to her sister and brushed her wet blonde hair from her face. "Bermuda, which way do we go? Are you able to sense Noah, or Perry?"

A bolt of lightning thundered down from the sky and struck the middle of the road behind them. Gravel was thrown into the air. Teleporting to the same place, Shane and Kathryn appeared.

The sisters turned and acknowledged the woman and their cousin.

"Girls," Kathryn gasped when she recognised the three blonde haired women in front of her. "Indy, Andy, Bermuda? How? Why are you three here?" She was obviously in a state of confusion.

Andromeda spoke, "Bermuda received a premonition a week ago."

Kathryn nodded. "Okay, but you need to be careful here, this world is dangerous..."

Bermuda cut her off with a sour look. "We figured that out when we were ambushed by Mangiare Demons in Penthal Manor, and hostile First Nations."

Kathryn showed concern. "Penthal Manor?"

"Yes," Isadora said before turning toward her sister. "Bermuda, you said you saw a ghost, but you didn't tell us the woman's name?"

Bermuda and Kathryn exchanged a silent, and secretive stare.

Aryan interrupted, drawing the group back to their original mission. "We came to Stanley Point because Bermuda is a Visionary too."

Kathryn seemed impressed. "Like Perry? Huh, fancy that."

The others dismissed her small talk. Becoming familiar again with the identity of the young Filipino witch, Kathryn remembered their meeting at Porteau Provincial Park when entering the Dream World. She'd been ambushed herself, along with Noah and Shane, by Mangiare Demons.

Kathryn apologized. "Aryan, forgive me. I'd almost forgotten your name. How did you come to find the three girls?"

Aryan replied, "Originally I had entered Prometheus's mind along with Kamenwati. We were at Gowlland Point fighting, after the devastation she brought upon Noah and Perry."

Bermuda murmured, "Devastation?"

"I was able to release the two he-witches from her influence, but when I was about to vanquish the demon, something or someone pulled her from this dimension." Aryan was obviously annoyed. "She got away unharmed."

Andromeda revealed the truth to the situation, "The Demon Paimon, was ordered to pull her out of this dimension, and back into the human world by Rafaela. Apparently, she was supposed to meet Rafaela in Nanaimo but never showed up."

Kathryn speculated, "That might explain why she attacked Shane in the forest near Ladysmith." The three sisters, along with Aryan, gave her an odd look. "Here in the Dream World. Rafaela was here with her Dark Promise Coven. But they were fought off, and banished by The Morrígan. Turns out." She turned her head and smirked at Shane. "Shane here is a Mischling!"

"What is the Dark Promise Coven?" Isadora asked, but it fell on deaf ears.

"So, he is like, Half Witch—Half Gypsy?" Andromeda asked with surprise.

"The Morrígan told me I was a gypsy in a past life, and I still have access to that part of myself," Shane revealed to his cousins.

Bermuda asked, "You actually met an Old One?"

"I swear on my own life," Kathryn said.

Bermuda wandered off into her own mind as the group continued to converse inaudibly to her ears. She was suddenly alerted to a male's voice. It was not the voice of Shane, who stood with the group.

The voice whispered in her ear, *"Bermuda, I need you."* Spinning around, she was greeted with a vision of Perry Pogue standing in the middle of the road. *"Bermuda, help me."*

Silently slipping away from the group, Bermuda walked up the gravel road toward the vision of her uncle.

His voice drifted toward her on the wind. *"Come to me, Bermuda Pogue."*

Bermuda recoiled when, for a split second, his eyes were filled with black. Black flames danced around his body. When his ominous visage disappeared, his eyes to their picturesque green. *"I need you Bermuda."*

Bermuda replied, "Perry, I will help you."

Kathryn conversed with the group, unaware of Bermuda's departure. "Isadora, it is good to see you back to your original hair colour."

Confused, Isadora frowned and pulled a piece of her long hair around to her line of sight. Her eyes bulged in dismay when she saw what was easily hidden in the human world, but worn openly in this world. Her hair was reinstated to its original colour, a beautiful blood red.

"Oh-oh, my-my god. Its red, it's supposed to be blonde," she stuttered, struggling to find the words.

Kathryn raised an eyebrow in curiosity. "You hate being a red head?"

Isadora pointed at Kathryn. "What about you? Your hair is charcoal grey. You're a Gray Witch, aren't you?"

Kathryn replied while toying with her long hair. "Yes I am. I am neither good, nor evil, but feared by both because I've been both at one point or more in my life. It is, what it is. One thing my dear is, you need to stop giving a crap about a lot of stuff including your hair. Wear it with pride, or don't wear it at all, I say. I am, what I am, and that's a bitch. I am good at it because people know where they stand with me."

Overhead, impressive bald eagles were circling without the group's knowledge.

Andromeda toyed at the idea Kathryn was preaching. "Bermuda, you know a thing or two about being a bit..." Turning, she was the first to acknowledge, her sister was no longer a part of the congregation. "Where did she go?"

Aryan turned and caught a glimpse of the young blonde-haired witch casually walking up Susan Point Road.

She pointed "There, where is she going?"

What everyone else saw as an empty gravel road, Kathryn – being a Gray Witch enabled certain abilities; like being able to perceive evil when others could not – could see a frail, and horrendous looking male individual clad in a black cloak which appeared to be made of black smoke.

"Hmm," she grumbled cautiously to herself, before commanding a Power Word Charm in Italian, "Rivelare! (Reveal)"as her hand shone blue with magic.

The air around Bermuda rippled as she moved, when it became still a moment later, a devilish looking male, who everyone could see, stood in front of her.

"Burke!!" Isadora screamed. "WHAT ARE YOU DOING?"

Swooping down from the sky, a large bald eagle squawked, and charged at the group causing them to shriek, and duck down to the gravel road. Soaring upward, the bird of prey spiralled and gave off a glow, shapeshifting into a levitating woman with feathers in her hair and clad in a white bra and brown skirt.

With a swing of her arm she projected several metal blades, made from her own feathers, down at the demon. Hitting the ground, multiple explosions threw gravel into the air. Bermuda gasped when a sharp wind blew her wet hair back. She shielded her face, and turned away. Bursting from the bushes at the road side, a fully-grown Buck leapt through the air, and landed on the road ahead of them. Letting out a territorial groan, it swayed its head. Its impressive antlers shone, and it fired two horn-shaped missiles at the demon.

Bermuda gasped, as the glowing objects hurtled toward her "Oh god, I'm going to die."

Whistling through the air, the projectiles passed by either side of her. She watched as the vision of Perry became impaled before exploding in a brilliant light.

Scrambling back to her feet, Isadora was bewildered by the thing before her. "Is that what I think it is?" She looked to Andromeda for conformation, "It's a fricken deer, isn't it?"

Andromeda replied sarcastically, "Wow, you're half as intelligent as I originally thought, Isadora. But, it would appear that it is a Buck, therefore a male."

Isadora grumbled irritably, "and you say Burke is a bitch, have you met yourself?"

Andromeda and her sister exchanged sour glares.

The Buck turned and spoke to the group, "I am Proud-Buck, Chief of the Forest Clan. Up there, is Grey-Wing, High Chief of the Bold Clan. You are not familiar with our world?"

Shane asked, "You're First Nations, aren't you?"

Andromeda murmured, "Shut up, show some respect."

The Proud-Buck ignored them and continued. "This world is treacherous, it cannot be trusted. Nightmare Soldiers, Mangiare, and Laedo stalk the shadows. It might be a world of dreams, and mirror the world you have come from, but it is also made of nightmares. If we had not heard you yell out her name, Bermuda would have been the next victim of that Laedo Demon."

"Laedo Demon?" Andromeda asked.

Proud-Buck nodded. "A Sub-sect of the Incubo Nightmare Soldiers, their name means incapacitate in Latin. They are considered to be more powerful than the Mangiare, who are the Dream Devourers. Laedo kill you by trapping you in your dreams, paralysing you by inserting their barb-like finger nails into your neck, and feed off your life force."

Bermuda spoke as she approached the group, "do you know where we can find Noah and Perry Pogue? The demon Kamenwati brought them here."

Proud-Buck turned his head and looked over his wither at her.

"Please, will you help us rescue them?"

Levitating down from the air, Grey-Wing, the female bald eagle first nation woman, landed on the gravel near the group. Kathryn stepped aside allowing Grey-Wing to halt beside Proud-Buck.

Grey-Wing pointed to a set of gates leading toward a private property. "At the end of this road, there is a manor. The Laedo are inside, they are strongest of the Nightmare Soldiers and have your kin."

A distraught Bermuda replied, "What about the visions I keep seeing? Are they dead?"

Grey-Wing closed her eyes, using her powers to feel, and sense the air she reopened them and looked at the witch before her.

"I do not sense death," she moved her head slightly and the wind elevated her long white hair. Gesturing her hand, she revealed her magic as golden energy sparkled in her right hand. With the energy, she was able to read Bermuda's aura "However, I do sense the Laedo used his powers to lure you here. He has marvellous abilities which allow him to exploit Kindred Spirits."

Isadora spoke up, "I say, let's exploit him."

~*~

Impressive evergreen forest stood on both sides of the tall iron gates of the property at the end of Susan Point Road. The mortal owners had creatively designed the road-side opening of their property to resemble interwoven metal vines.

Thunder rumbled in the grey, rainy clouds overhead.

Kathryn, Aryan and Shane stood curiously looking over the entry, pondering and cautious of whether or not there was an enchantment preventing them from crossing the threshold. A

Threshold Hex, – first created by Theodora Heldren of Salem, in the seventeen-hundreds – when executed by a magical individual, had the potential of killing a good, or evil, witch instantly when stepping foot onto a protected establishment.

Grey-Wing and Proud-Buck had departed, returning to their respectful clans of the forest and sky. Moving his arm and gesturing his hand at the gates, Shane spoke a Power Word Charm in Latin and his hand shone blue with magical energy.

"Aperi! (Open)"

Groaning, the gates parted, swung inward, and halted with just enough room for a person to walk between them. Uncertain, Shane lifted his leg and dangled his foot over the threshold. Smirking, Kathryn nudged him, causing him to lose his balance and stagger forward, revealing no dangerous magical enchantments.

"After you," she said courteously,

Shane ventured between the gates. "I don't know if I trust you."

"Don't start now," she toyed.

They moved cautiously down the driveway as it curved to the left until the front garden of a contemporary two storey manor, which overlooked the sea, came into view. Antique Victorian lamps scattered about the manicured lawn area, and forest edge, were alight and adorned with shrubs at their base. Beyond, on the ocean in the Strait of Georgia, was an impressive tall ship. The Nautica, a Pirate ship captained by Haarlem Blackheart.

Quietly, Kathryn, Shane, and Aryan, halted at the front door and hesitated. What would be beyond the door?

Inside the house, in the sunroom overlooking the ocean, soft light shone in as grey rain clouds refused to move on. There were two male bodies resting on white leather lounges side by side, but metres apart. A figure, dressed in a very baggy cloak, stood in the middle of the two bodies with its arms extended, and hands gestured over their heads.

Glittering grey energy emanated from the figure, and washed over the faces of Noah and Perry Pogue, as the Laedo incapacitated them, and trapped them in a deep slumber.

Removing its hood, the individual from behind was very broad across the shoulders, and had shaggy blonde hair. The Laedo's voice was familiar, and male. "Into dreams where shadows dwell, succumb to the power which is mine. No longer may you have the will to speak, under my control your strength shall weak."

Glancing ahead the individual saw himself in the mirror.

"Look what we have here." He toyed chauvinistically, but almost feminine with his mannerism. "A mortal, weak and pathetic, trapped inside a mirror. I could use and wear your body as I see fit for the rest of my life."

A ghostly mist swirled in the mirrors glassy surface, and an almost identical version appeared. The only difference, man in the mirror had amber coloured eyes compared to the blue ones of the man standing before the reflective piece of decor on the wall.

His voice was muted, but he could hear every word being said.

Chapter Nine

AS YOU WERE

Swaying his arm at the window, and gesturing his hand, he teleported a woman into the room. "Finally, sister, we have them where we want them. It seems almost anti-climactic, doesn't it?"

The woman with long black hair stood poised and beautiful. "Rasima, we can finally have our revenge."

Outside the room, on the other side of the locked doors to the sunroom, Andromeda, Bermuda, and Isadora stood hand in hand. In unison, they cast their spell. "In depths of dark, shadows bind, our power reaches out through space and time."

In the sunroom, as the woman stepped toward the two brothers, the windows behind her suddenly exploded, and the wind from outside blew the shards of glass into the room. Swiftly extending his arm, and directing his hand at the pieces of glass, the figure spoke an enchantment in Latin.

"Vacate. (Be still)"

The air and energy surrounding the woman warped, and distorted. She stood frozen in time, along with innumerable pieces of glass floating around her body in mid-air.

Lowering his free arm, he looked around the room for the presence of another with magical powers.

Outside the doors, the three sisters continued their spell. "We call arms, the goddess Nike, aid us in our time of need, obliterate what obscures thee."

The foundations began to quake, every window shattered, allowing wind to flow throughout the house. What a vision of potency, and strength, the three of them were with their concentrated expressions. The walls groaned.

Extending an arm each, the sisters commanded, "Everto!! (Obliterate)" in Latin.

The wall was demolished in a mighty explosion, and a cloud of dust filled the house. In the semi ruined sunroom, Perry's unconscious body, and Noah's mortally wounded form lay strewn on the floor. The woman, who had been summoned to the house, was propelled through a broken window, and onto the lawn. The figure, hidden conveniently beneath his cloak, lay on the floor.

The three sisters stepped over the rubble of the demolished wall, and entered the sunroom like noble warriors. Andromeda ventured further in, leant down, and attempted to tend to Noah's neck wounds. Bermuda halted in the middle of the room, and analysed the destruction.

Off to Bermuda's side, with her long red hair blowing in the wind, Isadora stood with her hands held upward, and conjured sparkling light in them. Light shone around her as she cast a summoning spell. "Gather to me, here and now, light of day, empower…"

Without warning, the cloaked figure levitated onto its feet, and stood with its back to the girls. Bermuda observed its movement closely, and Isadora was ready to attack should it strike first.

Lying on the grass outside, in full view of the shattered windows, the woman regained consciousness and lifted her head. Sighting Andromeda, she gasped and began to panic, fearing she would be seen, or worse, found out.

In Latin, she cast a spell upon herself. "Revertimini ad me, et veni in mundum. (Return me to the world I came from)" She was teleported from the Dream World in a small eruption of black smoke.

The figure growled under his cloak when he sensed the woman's sudden departure. "You are pathetic, sister. I will defeat the witches. You insolent girls think you know what power is?" His arm shot out, and he flicked his hand. Black bolts of lightning were directed at Andromeda as she knelt beside Noah's body.

"Andromeda! " Bermuda shrieked.

Turning her head, and observing the danger, Andromeda raised her hand. Rigidly gesturing, she projected a barrier of energy to keep the demonic attack at bay. Her body trembled as her power struggled against his. "Ugh," she groaned. "He is strong."

The black bolts of lightning, like snakes, viciously struck, and with every jolt seemed to become stronger. Exercising her power of Sensazione, Bermuda closed her eyes, a focused expression passed over her face and when she reopened her eyes, the pupil in each iris enlarged drastically. Using the Empathy branch of her power, she successfully hindered his power by blocking his nervous system, stopping the brainwaves from travelling to his hand, and gave it instruction.

"Now it's my turn. Oi!" Isadora stepped forward and threw a bolt of light at the cloaked individual. "Darth Maul." She mocked his similarity to the phantom menace of Star Wars, due to his true face being hidden beneath a cloak. Striking him in the side, she retorted, "let *me* show *you*, what power is." He was lifted and spun from the force of the attack before being slammed into the ground. "I am the witch of light, conqueror of..."

Isadora was cut-off mid-sentence when she was projected backwards by his telekinesis, and came to halt, slammed against one of the remaining walls of the room.

Startled, Bermuda's pupils decreased to their normal size. She lost her magical control over his hands as he revealed his mental abilities. He levitated from the ground, spun in the air, and the self-made breeze elevated his cloak, revealing his business suit attire beneath.

"I am Ima. Laedo, chief warrior of Kamenwati, and loyal worshipper of the godly Rafaela..." His voice was deep and masculine, appealing in a way.

Bermuda shouted, "oh god, shut up. I'm going to stop you right there." He fell silent and she continued, " I didn't like your pompous, arsehole nature when I walked in, and it still hasn't grown on me."

Outraged, he extended his arm, and projected black bolts of lightning toward her.

Lifting her arm, and holding her hand outward, she activated her power of Deflection; revealed in a brilliant golden glow. With a brisk wave, the lightning coiled off in various directions, striking and blasting holes in the ceiling and remaining walls.

Screaming, Andromeda tucked her body into a ball on the floor.

He appeared not to be impressed. "Cool parlour trick, witch."

Isadora muttered a banishing spell, "shadows crawl, small and tall, within light, becoming slight, I cast you out."

"Tsk, tsk, tsk," he hissed beneath his cloak. "Do you think I am so easily removed? I am not a shadow, you half-wit-witch. You can gain entry into this dimension simply by possessing a slumbering person. Or, remove them from their body, like I did with this meat sack."

"Bermuda," Shane yelled,

Turning, Bermuda caught a glimpse of Shane, Kathryn, and Aryan as they stood on the other side of the rubble.

The cloaked figure turned his attention to the three newcomers, and with his extended arm, telekinetically rebuilt the wall to keep the others out.

"NO!" Shane yelled, as he slammed his fist against the door which suddenly obstructed his view. "Curabit ut si quid obstat, (Obliterate what obstructs)" he commanded in Latin.

Kathryn gasped, and knowing the consequences of his actions, reached for his forearm. "Shane, no!"

Unfortunately, it was too late.

Shane, Kathryn, and Aryan were thrown backward by a brilliant blast of light and energy as an invisible barrier counteracted his spell.

On the other side of the room, the air rippled, and a vibrant, glowing portal comprised of watery energy, opened. Passing through it, the three witches were returned to the mortal world when Julyanne exercised her power from the security of her own home.

~*~

Ima, tormented the three sisters. "Any attempt you could have potentially made, to secure your future, and its safety are no longer feasible. Kamenwati turned Prometheus against Noah, and now the greatest of evils will return." He recited a small prophecy, "and the brothers shall take up arms. The Visionary will be the key, and when the fallen takes his last breath, he will breathe the beast's name, and the future of all evil will be secured."

Bermuda glanced to the side, a gasp left her lips when she noticed the wound on Noah's neck from where Perry had attacked him.

Shane's voice boomed from behind Ima, "prophecies are the thing I hate most."

Grabbed, and thrown to the middle of the room, the cloaked figure turned his head and looked back.

"You're gullible if you believe the future cannot be changed." Shane stood tall, broad shouldered, and proud. "The future is not final. So, if the next words out of your mouth are, 'we are evil, we are legion,' I might just make your future more fixed, and unpleasant than you'd care to imagine."

A dazed Ima replied, "Mm. Cocky little witch, aren't you?"

Extending his arm, the cloaked demon attempted to throw bolts of black lightning at Shane.

Quick to extend his own arm, and hand, Shane zapped the evil figure with his own power of Electrokinesis.

Andromeda rose to her feet. "The four of us, against the likes of him. I think it's time we showed this worthless idiot who has power, and who does not."

Isadora stood with her hands extended over Ima's shoulders, glimmering light within them. "*You* sought to pick a fight with us, Laedo. You lured Bermuda here, and knew damn well we'd follow. There was a time when we Pogue struck fear in demons, and all evil, alike. We were quiet for a while, but get ready, because we're making a comeback." She allowed her power of Photokinesis to flow through her entire body, and her aura glowed brightly."

Together the four of them cast their spell, "Venite, inquit, ad me, Ego sum lux, vos vento urente. (come to me, come to me, I am the light, you are the blight.)"

"Sorry, you're not killing me today. I still have secrets to say and blood to shed."

Swinging his arm out, the figure stopped time with a mere hand gesture. Sensing the strength of their united power, Ima, rose and as his body spun on the spot, it erupted into a black smoky mass. He fled, teleported back to the mortal world.

The four witches looked at one another with perplexed expressions on their faces. Bermuda straightened her back, and lifted her head, giving a look of superiority. Her hair floated on the wind blowing in through the broken windows. "We have company," she revealed. Her power of Sensazione acknowledged an invisible presence over her left shoulder. "Who?" The next words died on her lips, surprised by what she was seeing.

Entering the room from the area behind Bermuda, the dream god, Phantasos, brother of Morpheus, in his stark naked glory, had ventured down from his heavenly perch within the Dream World to inspect the damage inflicted upon Perry and Noah Pogue.

Isadora looked about, "I don't see anything."

Andromeda gave her twin sister a suspicious stare, "A ghost?"

"If you want to call it that." Bermuda spoke without thinking, or knowing, if Phantasos could hear her. "There is a naked man here."

He halted instantly and looked back at her.

"Ooops.." Her sisters, and Shane appeared confused. "Yeah, he heard me."

"You can see me?" Phantasos asked.

Bermuda laughed. " I am talking to you, aren't I?"

"You need to leave. The longer you linger here in the Dream World, the greater the risk, Noah will pass over to the other side. He has already begun the journey, and this was not his destiny."

Bermuda replied with surprise, "really? Without them?"

"What?" Isadora replied curiously.

Andromeda also wanted to know. "What did he say, the naked man?"

Stepping away from her sisters, and cousin, Bermuda crossed the semi demolished room, and knelt down beside Noah. She examined his face, and her eyes were drawn to his neck wound when she moved his head slightly to the side. Turning her head, she glanced across at Perry who lay unconscious a few metres away.

"We don't possess anywhere near the kind of power needed to revive them. They were induced by that man, that figure," Bermuda admitted.

Phantasos began, "that man was..." Glancing toward the window, he noticed the ghost of Carmen Penthal giving him a strict hand gesture across her throat, implying he needed to be quiet, and say no more. "You will need a High Priestess to reverse this black magic."

Shane shouted, "we need Tempest Pogue."

Andromeda, Isadora, and Bermuda all looked at him quizzically, but they were quickly replaced with expressions of understanding. Beside Noah and Perry, and knowing the Romani were pre-occupied with searching for Brady Romani, Tempest was the only powerful witch they knew on both sides of living, and dead who knew how to reverse Nightmare Soldier Magic.

Phantasos cast his spell, "I return you to the world from whence you came."

Emitted from his naked body, a brilliant light washed over the room, and eclipsed the four witches, Noah and Perry Pogue; immediately they were transported from the Dream World, and returned to the Human World.

In the fading light, two more figures revealed themselves in the sunroom of the manor with Phantasos. Morpheus stood proud, naked and masculine; another brother Phobetor was equally as broad shouldered, and proud in his naked glory. Opposite to them, before the broken windows, the Morrígan appeared.

The Morrígan spoke as one. "A great evil was committed in our realm. Spirits may come and go as they please to visit the human world, but from this point in time, no demon or witch, good or evil, shall be welcomed here. I am sealing the dimension off from foreign travellers."

Phobetor spoke, "what about the Haus of Romani in the further woods? I have foreseen it, they will want to return to it, bring it back to the mortal world."

The Morrígan replied in sync, "and, they shall have it. I will make contact with Queen Maria. As you were," the Persia Romani look-a-like swayed her hand in the air. "Return to your perch, the three of you."

Lowering their heads in respect, the three brother gods teleported out of the manor in glows of gold, and returned to their heavens above.

The Morrígan lingered for a moment longer, staring about the room, and inspecting the damage.

"Reparo! (Repair)"

In a wash of glittering golden energy, the ruin brought about by Ima to the beautiful manor on the coastline of Pender Island, was restored to its original and well-kept state.

RETURN OF THE GAMMA WITCH

T he weather over the city of Treadwell, Deane County was overcast with sunshine beaming down through small gaps where the clouds permitted. Thirty minutes east of the city, up the freeway through the Treadwell hills, the expanding country city of Summit Hills was under a heavy grey cloud of rain.

Rumbling in the sky implied Weather Being's anger, and then came the colossal explosion of thunder which rippled through the air. Lightning forked, and flashed, across the abyss of grey. Atop her plateau, the beautiful woman stood with her arms extended; her eyes closed, and wind blowing in the gale.

"Worship me great city of Treadwell, for I am Corazón." She spoke to the city below, but her words died on the wind without being heard. Because of the evil in the area, the weather was becoming more corruptible, "I am a great thunder, I will lay waste to your–"

Interrupted by a crackling noise, followed by an explosion, she opened her eyes, and looked above her to see a portal of rippling energy open up. A thick beam of golden light, which resembled a comet plummeted down before the portal quickly closed. Watching it pierce through her cloud mass, and destroy it, Corazón let out a scream as she was vanquished in a blinding light.

~*~

In the attic of Aaron Pogue's house, his daughters Bermuda, Andromeda and Isadora, with the aid of their cousin Shane; stood outside a circle of white flame lit candles. They had positioned themselves in North, South, East, and West, as a clever measure to draw power from the nautical compass which was the symbolic power their father, Noah, and Perry had harnessed.

"Veniat ad me (Come to me), Veniat ad me (Come to me)." The four of them chanted the intro of their summoning spell in unison, and in Latin. "We cast our voice into the void; heed our call on the other side. Spirit of Tempest Pogue, we summon thee. Come to us and settle here."

Feeling the power of the compass, Bermuda, Andromeda, Isadora, and Shane gasped as it overcame them for a moment, and their eyes shone beautifully before returning to normal. The beam of falling golden light folded over the house before magically vanishing within the tiled roof.

Glittering orbs descended from the ceiling, to the floor, inside the circle. They levitated for a moment, before expanding, and taking the form of a ghost - a woman with long blonde hair dressed like Jill Munroe of Charlies Angels. She hovered before lowering to stand on the floor.

Tempest greeted her great-grandchildren. "Hello my darling great-grandchildren."

The four of them stared, confused.

Tempest turned and held her arms toward Bermuda. "I've been waiting for your call. My, you are quite powerful, Bermuda." As her eyes drifted over the four of them, she found she was impressed with the level of strength and ingenuity before her. " All of you are powerful in your own right, but Bermuda...." Tempest focused her attention back on the eldest of the four. "You will become the leader of this coven."

Isadora snapped, "we did not call you for an ego trip."

Tempest turned and acknowledged the radiant witch with her piercing eyes.

Isadora continued. "We need your help. When we last saw you, we were searching for Perry."

Tempest spoke, "Ah yes, I remember. You disappeared off the radar for months; I was not able to sense you from Santo Cathedral. Where have you been? Did you manage to locate Prometheus?"

"We located him in the Dream World, being held captive in an induced slumber which we are unable to break. Nightmare Soldier magic is proving to be extremely powerful here in the real world." Andromeda explained.

Shane elaborated. "So, that is why we summoned you, Tempest. The Romani are preoccupied with their troubles, and are unable to assist us. You're the only one powerful enough that we know of, who is capable of undoing what has incapacitated Noah and Perry."

Tempest understood, nodded and lifted her foot to step over the circle of candles to re-enter the real world again.

"Ah." Isadora waved her hand, manipulating the energy and light given off by the candles, to prevent her great-grandmother from leaving the circle. "We both felt, and saw the damage you were able to do last time. How can we trust the Gamma Witch power won't cause more destruction and chaos?"

Revealing the level of power she possessed, Tempest easily overpowered Isadora's magic, and stepped from the circle. Upon stepping onto the floor, her aura shone, and she assumed a full corporeal form. The flames atop the candles dissipated into a line of smoke.

Tempest smiled as she approached the Book of Shadows by the window. "Isadora, you are young, still very much untrained, and a little naive when it comes to power witchery. Gamma Power is a united power source. I cannot possess it singularly. I need my sisters to be with me to access it; hence the nature of Philomena, and my power with our last visit. I am here as a powerful witch, and High Priestess."

Shane approached hesitantly. "No chaos?"

"No destruction." Tempest chuckled as she flipped through the pages of the Book of Shadows; but suddenly halted her hands, closed the book, and looked up. "Before I can do anything, I need to see them. I need to know the severity of the afflictions Kamenwati put upon them."

Standing at the back of the room, on the farthest side of the circle of candles, Bermuda could hear whispering. It was distinct, different to the voices of anyone else in the room. Stepping carefully, and slowly to the side, with her head tilted and a curious look on her face, she acknowledged the presence of a noblewoman chatting in Tempest's left ear. She had brown hair done up beneath a fancy oversized hat, a Victorian-era gown, and captivating blue eyes.

"Be on your guard," she whispered sternly. "Something is off-putting in this house, and it isn't the cat."

Bermuda narrowed her eyes and spoke curiously, "what cat?"

Startled at being found out, the ghost of the woman both Tempest, and her great-granddaughter could see, gasped. She turned, levitated across the floor a few inches and faded quickly.

Isadora turned slightly. "I hate it when you do that. It makes me think twice about who the hell might be watching me get undressed. Is the ghost gone?"

Bermuda stared sarcastically at her sister.

Tempest smirked. "You, and I are similar my dear, Bermuda. I too am a medium. I too possessed the power of Sensazione. But I relinquished it due to our families' dramatic history involving the unique power which only twins seem to inherit. However, I am innately a medium as well as a Firestarter."

Andromeda, curious as always about the visitations of ghosts only Bermuda could see, asked a question just like every other time her sister revealed the presence of an invisible entity. "Who..."

Bermuda anticipated her sister's question. "A woman. By the clothing, I guess she was colonial era maybe, or even Victorian. I loved the hat. Very big, nice statement piece I thought."

Andromeda nodded, fascinated.

Tempest revealed the name of the ghost. "Amethyst. She is one of our many ancestors, and a witch. She was a member of the High Coven of Salem. Look in the book, do some research, learn about your heritage." Carrying the families Book of Shadows across the room, she halted at the door, and glanced back at the next generation of witches. "Shall we?" She gestured to the stairs leading down to both Perry and Noah.

Isadora, Bermuda, Andromeda, and Shane, nodded and crossed the attic toward her.

~*~

Tempest led the way down the stairs with Isadora at her side,

behind the others followed. At the foot of the staircase, the lower level came into immediate view. To the far right was the double front entry, modern doors with tempered glass inserts. Polished, floating floorboards flowed down the hallway. Directly opposite the staircase was a wall painted lavender with white skirting. A modern fireplace was accessible to the lounge room as well as the hall. Pendant ceiling lights, fixed in intervals gave the hallway a vintage charm.

Stepping off the staircase, Tempest shivered with the cold atmosphere of the house. She removed her hand from the Book in her grasp, waved her arm, and threw a small spark into the fireplace causing it to ignite with her power of Pyrokinesis.

"Why so cold?" she asked Isadora. "This is a beautiful house and it should be kept warm and welcoming, not unpleasant."

Pausing at the square archway into the lounge room, she gazed at Perry and Noah lying on sofas. "They look peaceful," she sighed sympathetically.

Aaron stood proud, his usual obnoxious self behind the armchair. "Grandmother, what are you?" He was surprised to see her, and addressed her formally. He acted like a child who had been interrupted doing something naughty. "Why-why are you here?" His amber eyes narrowed. "Isadora, what is the meaning of this?"

Tempest raised an eyebrow; shocked at his attitude towards her, and his children.

He stared at Tempest without speaking further, attempting to intimidate her. "You usually greet guests in such a manner? You weren't born stiff, so don't start acting it now, boy. Your mother and I raised you to be a man, not an arse."

She placed the Book of Shadows onto the coffee table as she entered the room, and moved to carefully touch Perry, and Noah's faces, and necks.

Aaron's hawk eyes fixated on the book, Bermuda observed him without being noticed. It appeared he thought he could cause the book to burst into flames by merely looking.

Aaron growled at his three daughters, "Who summoned her? Answer me. You know I hate you using witchcraft, it is nothing but poison. Which of you should I reprimand?" He glared at the sisters, ignoring Shane as if he wasn't there.

Andromeda slammed her hands on her hips and glared back at her father. She had certainly inherited his arrogance. "I'd like to see you try, old man. What kind of father thinks he can reprimand his adult children? Seriously, you continue to become more, and more absurd."

Amethyst reappeared at Tempest's side, and whispered into her ear. Leaning to the side, hearing and taking note, Bermuda observed the ghost, but this time did not make its presence known.

"There is paint over the circle," Amethyst said. "Do mirrors usually talk? Is that normal?"

Tempest turned, and peered at the mirror mounted on the wall. Turning back, she looked down and removed her hand from Noah's face, and neck. She nodded as she listened to the ghost talking in her ear.

Aaron spoke in a derogatory manner, "I see you still nod your head, Tempest. Always thought you were crazy when you said ghosts were talking to you."

Tempest glared at him, but remained silent as she ventured back to the Book of Shadows on the coffee table. She turned to face him once she had the book in her grasp. "Give me one good reason why I don't magically remove your penis from your groin, and place it on your forehead?"

"You know the rules in my house, Tempest. No magic. I relinquished that part of my life which brought only destruction."

Ravenna, Aaron's alcoholic wife entered the room with a glass of whiskey in her hand.

Tempest spoke sarcastically, "what about this destructive force?"

Ravenna stood beside her husband. "Oh, look dear, Mary Poppins has arrived."

Tempest replied, "I'd watch your mouth dear, my grandson has always been too good for you. What time is it?" She glanced at her watch. "It's not even past nine am and you're already on the alcohol."

Andromeda growled with a scolding expression, "this is why I moved to Canada."

Standing in the doorway, Bermuda ignored everything happening around her, and curiously observed the ghost of Amethyst as she chatted inaudibly in Tempest's ear. But then, by accident, the Telepathy branch of her Sensazione power overheard whispering thoughts between Aaron, and Ravenna. Both cleverly engaged in verbal conversation with Tempest, and Andromeda while engaging in mental chatter with one another.

Aaron could not possess magic or the power of telepathy; he said he'd relinquished his magic years ago?

"The mirror seems to have slipped their sight," Ravenna said.

Aaron replied, "Good, keep it that way."

But, while she observed her parents inconspicuously she also became aware, for a male, his thoughts were female in voice rather than manly. Glancing to her left, she caught a quick glimpse of the mirror mounted on the wall to her side. Before she could step further into the room to have a closer look, a ghost in the hallway caught her attention.

Aaron spoke rudely, "So, old woman, how you are going to bring the two of them back? You're a ghost." His sarcasm was rife, and rude. For a supposedly *old* woman, Tempest did not look a day over fifty. "You possess no...."

Then, without warning, while reading the book, she extended an arm at her grandson, and commanded an incantation in Italian. "Silenzio!"

Taken aback by her skill, Aaron attempted to talk but found he had no voice.

Tempest shouted, "for the life of you, shut up! Because, I will forcibly remove your fricken tongue if you continue to be so rude." She glanced at him from the pages of the book. "I'm going to use the Restoration Spell, it's somewhere in the book."

Placing the book down on the coffee table, she held her hand over the open pages. Closing her eyes, she spoke in Latin. "Invenietis (find me)." A breeze blew the pages until they finally halted, and the aged pages fell flat. "Ah, here we go. Our ancestor, Amethyst Forrestal wrote this spell, 'To Restore One from Darkness'. It says we need to lay the suffering person, or persons, in a circle made of white candles."

Isadora queried, "But, that's the same way we summoned you."

"Bathed in light," Shane began to give his opinion, "the infected evil is driven out of the body and soul."

Aaron moved uneasy as he listened.

Shane continued, "Grandma. Does it say to place Lavender, Rose Petals, and salt over the body?"

Tempest nodded her head, trailing her finger along the paragraph as she silently read. She did not reply at first, but upon finishing reading, she lifted her head, and spoke to her great-grandson over her shoulder. "Who taught you how to perform this incantation?"

Shane replied nervously, "my mother said she had to use it on a friend once."

Turning away, Tempest studied Perry, and murmured cautiously to herself. She knew Connemara had performed the spell on him when Caydit turned him into a vampire, but it proved unsuccessful because he had already fed on human blood to consummate his transition.

Chapter Eleven

WHERE IS MY SON?

Sunlight peeked through small openings in the grey clouds over the city of Treadwell.

For the moment, the wind was gone, and it looked like the wintery weather, in the middle of summer, was finally departing. There was a clear and noticeable rumble of thunder, and the breaks in the grey clouds rejoined, blocked out the beautiful blue, and the sky became charcoal and ominous.

On top of Treadwell's tallest skyscraper, the thirty-one storey, Gainsborough Bank building; Pilar, Siobhan, Juliann, and Zane cast a spell. Drawing on weather deities, they used thunder to disturb the atmosphere around any invisible magics. But then, using lightning, the disturbed magic would act as a lightning rod pinpointing Brady Romani's possible location.

Pilar stood near the edge, while her siblings stood a little further behind her. She cast a summoning spell, "From the sky the power came, into the ground, for none to have, and none to reign."

Siobhan called out as the fierce wind blew around her, "Pilar, the Hellmouth will not yield to you."

Pilar repeated the spell.

Juliann yelled to her sister over the wind. "Its power is too strong, Pilar. No one can control the Hellmouth."

Pilar's strength as a mother emanated from her in kinetic energy as she willed deities associated with wind, thunder, rain, and sky. "Aura, Thor, Indra, Aide, I summon the power which resides. Power beneath thy city home, only to borrow, not to own."

"PILAR! " Zane shouted frantically.

The clouds directly overhead became darker than the grey rain clouds blanketing the sky over the city. A mighty boom of thunder cracked directly overhead. Along King Gustav Boulevard the iron manhole covers rocketed into the air, causing traffic to screech to a halt as the supernatural influenced storm bored down on the city, and its mortal citizens.

An otherworldly, disembodied groan moved through the city.

Juliann was paralysed with fear. "What the hell is that?"

Released from the holes in the street, watery- blue, mystical energy of the Hellmouth overcame Pilar, and her siblings as it took momentary possession of them. The energy possessed Zane, and as Ryder Romani exited a building in Treadwell's, Logan Square, she gasped.

Stiffening her posture as though struck in the back, Ryder closed her eyes, and was instantly teleported to another plane of existence.

~*~

*I*t was not so long ago, while in the Treadwell Botanical Gardens

with her cousins fighting Visper, the newly sired Philanderer Demon, under the possession of her master Saxon Preston – Ryder, had called upon the power of the Triad's sacred Triple Goddess to aid her in banishing the overlord from the newborn demon.

Intentionally using the power to save, and protect her relatives, Ryder had unwittingly allowed herself to become a conduit to the sacred power. Wearing the Solar Star Talisman amplified her call tenfold, convincing the deity the Romani was

111

worthy of its power. The same power her father - Zane, and the Triad drew on to enhance their own magic.

The role of the conduit, which was once Zane, and now his daughter, was to anchor the immense power of the Triad to the earth. Without him or her, their ultimate power, as well as their telepathy, had the probability of killing them.

Letting out a shriek, Ryder reappeared in the Bocca dimension; a place of perpetual white. A disembodied groan resonated as something colossal made its presence felt. Silence immediately followed.

"Where am I?" Ryder asked surrounding air.

The disembodied groan sounded again, this time louder as though right beside her. Shrieking again, she covered her ears with her hands, and hunched over. There was primordial force here, and its power filled every fibre of her being like a billion volts of electricity. Her body felt like it was being shredded into thousands of tiny pieces.

Behind her, far away in the distance, Astral Projections of the Triad appeared, and the three of them cast their summoning spell, "From the sky the power came, into the ground, for none to have and none to reign."

Ryder gasped aloud with relief as the immense pain subsided, and the disembodied groan returned for a moment. Glancing over her shoulder, she glimpsed four figures. But, then her attention was drawn to something mammoth in size directly ahead of her.

"Aura, Thor, Indra, Aide, we summon the power that resides, power beneath thy city home, only to borrow, not to own," the triad thundered in unison.

Stepping forward, Ryder raised her arm. "Reveal to me what remains unseen." Casting a spell, coupled with a gesture of her hand, a golden glow revealed half of an enormous, watery-blue, sphere. "What the hell is that?"

The disembodied groan returned. Within the sphere a massive prehistoric whale-like creature breached and the mystical, water substance containing it suddenly erupted, and showered the white dimension in blue. Shrieking, Ryder turned, and shielded herself with her arms from the tidal wave of watery energy.

A blue, featureless and watery figure levitated before the young Romani, and although it was unseen, acknowledged the Solar Star Talisman around her neck. Deeming her worthy of its colossal power, the manifestation of the Hellmouth surged forward, and entered the conduit's body.

~*~

The wind atop the Gainsborough Bank building howled like a banshee as it vigorously blew Pilar's long, brunette hair about. She stood with her eyes closed for a moment as she felt herself; Siobhan, Juliann, and Zane connect with the power of the Hellmouth.

In perfect synchronization, they reopened their eyes, and revealed blue mystical power. With a brisk elevation of her arms, Pilar and the Triad began to successfully wield the power of the Hellmouth. From her hands, and fingertips, she projected bolts of marvellous blue lightning at the storm directly overhead.

Extinguishing her magic, Pilar lowered her arms.

Lightning flashed and forked across the sky.

Raising her arm swiftly upward at the sky, Juliann, her eyes full of blue power, projected her power of Pulse Manipulation. Kinetic energy rippled from her hands as it moved quickly up, and into the clouds. She commanded, "disturb now as you intertwine. Reveal all hidden magics to me, and mine."

A mighty eruption of thunder pursued upon the activating of Juliann's spell. Dispersing her power of Pulse Manipulation, the thunder cast ripples from the sky, and revealed a glittering blanket of invisible magic which covered not only the city of Treadwell, but the entire Deane County.

Extending her arm, Siobhan, her eyes filled with blue power of the Hellmouth, activated her power of Pyrokinesis. She emitted a bellowing roar, and the immediate air around her mouth rippled with kinetic energy as she breathed a torrent of flames. From the torrent, wings reached out, and flapped. Siobhan closed her mouth, and deactivated her power.

Enhanced by the power of the Hellmouth, as the flames flew away from the building, they magically morphed into a large and fiery phoenix. Super charged, Zane reached his right arm forward, and was able to project his Astral Speed power in the form of green astral energy. Absorbed into the fiery creature it turned from red to emerald.

"VIA!" the four commanded with a brisk wave of their hands, They cast a small incantation in Italian, "Ora prendere il volo (Now take flight)." As one, in english, they spoke, "Find. Locate. Reveal to us the evil which has abducted one of our own." They sent the fiery creature off.

Letting out an ear-piercing squawk, the spectacle flapped its flaming wings, and shot upward into the storm clouds where it disappeared in a brilliant glow.

~*~

"*Y*ou have proven yourself worthy," spat an enormous voice.

Ryder replied, "What I am worthy of?" She groaned slightly, her insides felt like they were being twisted. "Ugh." She bent forward, placed a hand on her stomach, and whispered the name of her ancestor. "Amedea, help me."

Feeling a warm, soothing hand caress the left side of her face, she felt healed.

The enormous voice returned, "worthy of my power."

Ryder straightened. "Who are you? Reveal yourself."

Her eyes shone a powerful blue in response to her demand.

"I am within you," replied the voice, almost male-like. "I am the power you summoned. I have no physical form, I just am."

Ryder nodded. "You're the Hellmouth."

The booming voice asked, "Do you know what happened to the last witch who tried to siphon my power?"

Without warning, Ryder let out an agonizing scream and turned her face upward. She held her arms out, and arched her back. Brilliant bolts of blue electricity gripped her body as the Hellmouth executed its ultimate power upon her. Proving, its power cannot be contained, it was a force all of its own.

~*~

Atop the Gainsborough Bank in downtown Treadwell, the Triad stood powerful as they glared into the distance, waiting for the fiery phoenix to reveal the location of Brady Romani.

The first to feel the immense power surge of the Hellmouth within them, Zane let out a cry of pain, and buckled down to one knee.

Combusting in her hands, Siobhan was next to let out a scream. Flames spiraled up from around her feet to her hips, and catapulted her backward into the wall.

"I am not yours to contain. No witch or gypsy shall have power over me," spat a demeaning, deep, and male-like voice.

Juliann screamed, "PILAR! "

A sudden flash of light threw Pilar backward into her sister. Sitting upright, and quickly reaching her arm forward at the area in front she gestured her hand rigidly, her eyes full of blue power. "By power and might, I bind your power until I recite...."

The booming voice responded, "You cannot control me Mischling."

"THY WILL BE DONE, MY WISH IS ONE, FIND ME MY SON!" Pilar's shout had a magical reach so strong, her voice cast concussive waves of energy.

The booming voice let out a roar of agony as it bent to her will. Suddenly, there was a mighty explosion behind the clouds, followed by a brilliant flash of crimson light. A wave of kinetic energy was cast out from the Bocca Dimension by the Hellmouth, fanned out across the city of Treadwell, and then even further, across the entire Deane County. Any invisible magic, good or evil, was momentarily disrupted.

Reacting to Pilar's powerful magic, and expelled from Ryder's body, the magical manifestation of the Hellmouth, as sparkling molecules; resumed the watery and featureless form once more. "You shall know where the boy is kept."

In the real world, choked by the heavy storm overhead, the fiery phoenix and magic of the Triad, reappeared some miles off in the distance. Its glowing form plummeted from the clouds over the mountains hemming in Treadwell. Drawing on their united magic, Pilar peered into the distance, and as she did, her pupils dilated as her vision distorted around the edges, and accelerated forward. Her long hair flapped in the wind.

The towering steeples of Eris rose up between the two peaks of Castambul, and Paracombe of the Rune Mountains in the distance. Its protective, glittering magical shield collapsed as a result of the spell cast by the Triad to disrupt all local, invisible magic. The protective invisible magic hiding the evil, and gothic medieval city, was for a moment, useless.

"Hide in your fortified city, Morgana. But, I will move the earth, and level Eris." Pilar was godly with intimidating blackened eyes. "Those dwelling above ground have had it too good for too long."

Treadwell felt her fury. A pulse of kinetic energy was expelled from her body.

Expressed into the Bocca Dimension, Pilar's pulse of kinetic energy was expelled from Ryder's body. Levitating opposite the young Romani, the manifestation of the Hellmouth let out a bellowing roar. Reaching its arm forward it ruthlessly banished Ryder from the Dimension as its figure was abruptly, and painfully dispersed

Chapter Twelve

PHANTOM

It was a busy month in Treadwell City. With the Festival month underway, the mortal citizens were out enjoying the nightlife while the climate was warm before winter arrived in town. Everyone knows winter in Treadwell is bitter: -5 degrees, a steady snowfall and occasional heavy rain.

The innocent and ignorant were easy pickings tonight.

In the Evoke Bar, on King Gustav Boulevard, a woman danced to 70's disco song *Feels like I'm in Love* by *Kelly Marie* amongst other mortals at the bar's rear. Euphoria was aloft, and time appeared to move slowly around each, and every sleek movement of her versatile body.

Leaning against the bar, a man, perhaps in his early to mid-thirties, eyed off the flirtatious woman while drinking a pint of beer. He was tall, neatly dressed in his black pants and royal blue shirt. Stubble complimented his square jaw. Brown eyes of his caught her green ones, and a seemingly intimate connection was instantly made.

Smiling seductively, while dancing and swirling around, the woman let him know he had captured her attention, She stopped suddenly, and a bold look crossed her face, as she strode toward him confidently. Her long blonde hair blew before she halted directly in front of him.

She smiled at him as she asked, "want to see, what I can do?"

He stared at her, captivated.

Reaching her arms forward, she placed her hands on his head, and he suddenly cried out in agony. Magically, the scenery of the Evoke Bar rippled like water, and morphed into the Meat Locker Catacombs which the evil Old One – Eisheth, had once occupied, but had since abandoned after being banished by Ryder Romani.

Standing opposite him, in the void of white, Kamenwati worshipped him as he hung on butcher's hooks. "Torture is one of my many talents. It appeared you actually enjoyed me recreating the night we first met."

Weakened, he murmured, "What do you want with me?"

She smirked. Brushing stray curls back behind her ear, she stepped forward to his side. She gestured at her possessions on an altar before them. A large cauldron, several black candles, herbs, spices, and various potion ingredients required to create a nasty concoction. With her free hand, she caressed the side of his hung head, and tenderly ran her fingers through his thick brown locks. Gripping them hard, she pulled his head up, and growled in his ear.

"There are six hundred and sixty-five victims within these catacombs. You make six hundred and sixty-six. Eisheth was going to slaughter the Romani girl but she proved too powerful. But you, Andros, will be the witch to replace the one who got away."

He spoke huskily, "how-how do you know I'm a witch?"

She dropped his head unceremoniously and crossed to her altar "Because you reek of goodness. To us demons, it's a tardy, vinegar taste in our mouth, where you taste honey. Plus, I've been stalking you. You possess the power of Matter Alteration. You can use mirrors as portals." Kamenwati brought her hands down to rest on her altar. "Shall we begin?"

Although significantly weakened from being tortured for innumerable days, Andros attempted to struggle free from the hooks holding him. Placing her hands into jars, and bowls,

Kamenwati smirked at his attempts while taking pinches of this, and that, placing them into her cauldron.

"Hear now the mother." She began to cast a spell. "Her wisdom like no other. Authority of the father, a demon and survivor." A spark flashed, a small explosion echoed within the cauldron as her words, and ingredients reacted. "Into the dark, of worlds uncharted, I cast my call, bring her to me. Blessed be Alera."

Falling silent while she focused on her enchantment, and placing himself into an unconscious state, Andros used another power in his arsenal to create a clone. Staggering away at a hurried pace from the Nightmare Soldier, he extended his arm in a flurry, waved his hand, and summoned a mirror to his location. The raw emotion displayed on his face showed he was frantic for freedom, and home.

"So long," he murmured to himself, wincing in pain. "Bitch!"

Stepping through the mirror, the reflective surface slipped over him like silk. Emerging on the other side, he let out an instant, uncomfortable groan. Blood spilled from the corner of his lips. Glancing down he noted an arm reaching into his chest. Lifting his head, he was greeted by beautiful, and startling Rafaela. He groaned uncomfortably again. She gave him a cold glare, pulled her bloodied arm from his chest, and watched as he dropped dead to the ground. In her hand, she cradled his still beating heart.

~*~

Hearing the commotion behind her as she tended to her dark ritual, Kamenwati peered over her shoulder, and silently observed. Her superior had teleported into the dimension without her knowledge.

Rafaela spoke while Kamenwati stood in the background, "a witch's power is tied to their emotions, emotions are tied to the heart. So, does that mean the heart is the power we all possess?"

Turning on the spot, the entire catacombs felt insignificant to her beauty, and power. She wore a fantastic black gown composed of different fabrics. Grey silk gloves up to her elbows, a theatrical fascinator over one side of her face, and beautiful gazelle horns amongst long dark hair.

Kamenwati answered, "makes sense, the heart is your core. Therefore, your mind contains all your fears, all your nightmares." She picked up a glass vial containing an opaque substance. "Ask Perry Pogue, his mind is a gold mine."

Maintaining strict eye contact, Rafaela approached her most accomplished demon – the only one in her court to actually do any significant damage to the Pogue Witches – she appeared to levitate around the altar before halting directly opposite.

She and Kamenwati exchanged an odd stare, suspiciously caring for the likes of demons. "I will admit, Incubo, you are the only demon who manages to do any significant damage toward those bloody witches. The rest have only half-assed attempts."

Kamenwati objected. "Azazel and her brother Alistair are equally as good as me. I got Perry, but hey managed to..."

Rafaela gestured to the deceased bodies in their presence, and hissed cautiously, "do not ruin it. You don't know who might be listening. I'm eager to see how it will all play out."

Smirking, as she listened, Kamenwati's attention was secretly focused on the vial she held at eye level in the palm of her hand. Under her breath she was muttering almost inaudible words. Suddenly the opaque substance within glimmered before turning red.

"Jana, Dayea, goddess Vecna." The first verse of the spell called upon three deities associated with secrets. "I call upon your power; hear me in this sacred hour." Kamenwati poured the red substance into her cauldron. "Disentwine the secrets of the mind."

She dropped Hemlock into the concoction.

"Hemlock," Rafaela commented knowingly.

Kamenwati nodded. "I'm using it to reverse the spell the Sognare Coven put on Perry Pogue to stop the nightmares. They were clever, I'll give them that much. The opaque substance I turned red was those nightmares."

She swayed her hand over the cauldron with her eyes closed, and sensed all the magics intertwining with one another. "No wonder he couldn't sleep, I almost feel sorry for him. This is the work of legends; I could not wield this kind of power even if I tried."

Suddenly, a low disembodied groan flowed around the dimension. Intrigued Rafaela glanced about, and immediately identified the approaching juggernaut.

She turned slightly, appearing scared, and looked back at Kamenwati."I believe the Old Ones are trying to intervene, but it's against their religion."

The disembodied groan grew louder when it surfaced again.

Kamenwati growled, "let them try. It's common knowledge, they cannot interfere in any way, because it would bring about the wrath of their creators as well as the Sisters of Fate. Now, place the damn heart in the cauldron, we're going to use Andro's power to conjure a special kind of mirror."

An intrigued Rafaela replied, "Oh?"

~*~

Standing in her spacious, and superior office space in the Glacier Castle – a school constructed, and principled by Maria the Queen of Good Magic, to nurture good, juvenile witches – the Old Ones had gathered. Scattered about the upper level, they stood before the mammoth sized window which had the perfect, birds-eye-view of Treadwell, and Deane County.

"We are really going to stand here and..." asked an outraged Vulcan. He was broad across the shoulders, six-feet-tall, and dressed in a business suit. The kind of man you could stare at, just stare at, and lose track of time.

"You know the consequence of interfering," Aryan reminded him.

To the magical society of Mongkukulam, she was a witch. However, sometime during the seventeenth century, Aryan was left catatonic after a demon attack. Her mother, and powerful witch, Lilane, agreed to allow Vesta, the Old One she often prayed to, to merge with the spirit, and soul of her daughter, to bring her back from the brink of death.

All the Old Ones are able to walk the earth, and live mortalesque lives. Due to her merging with the witch, Vesta, is the only Old One with authorization to interfere in the battle between good and evil.

"Do as the pretty one says," snarled a familiar female voice.

Turning their attention away from the window, Minerva, Naberius, Anne the Great, Lilith, Lamia, Ceres, Mercury, Apollo, Lucia, Mars, The CEO, and Maria all looked upon three blonde haired, blue eyed, gorgeous women dressed in white.

Atropos, Lachesis, and Clotho, ultimate in their power, originated as part of the first race of man known as Hominis. They were the three original witches. Later, in world mythology, they would become known as the Aryan Race with their distinct blonde hair and blue eyes.

Sitting on the arm of the leather chair, Lachesis stared at the Old Ones. Atropos stood in the middle, and Clotho to her right with her arms folded.

"You know the cost for interfering?" Atropos glared at them, at the front line of supremacy in the universe, the Fates governed everything magical and mortal. "We dictate what comes to pass. You might be *older*, but we, my sisters and I, are more powerful. We could decide your fate right here, right now." The smug look on her face told more than she let on. They knew she was more than capable of removing them from the face of the earth. "Now you Neanderthals, the demon-bitch will summon the phantom mirror."

Clotho was firm. "Kamenwati and Rafaela will use the mirror to release Alera from the Dark Dimension."

Lachesis revealed the loophole. "Without the witch's heart, Alera is merely a phantom. Lindsay Pogue was buried without her heart for the very reason, that some half-cocked demon might resurrect, Alera."

In a flash of light, Atropos conjured a large antique book they used to transcribe events, lives, and deaths. Running her finger down the page, it was clear to see the depth of seriousness she placed on her occupation. "Captain Haarlem and his pirates have the heart on their ship, the Nautica. And..." she slammed the book shut. "only we three, and now you all know this minor detail."

~*~

The first verse of the spell called upon three deities associated with secrets. "Jana, Dayea, goddess Vecna, I call upon your power; hear me in this sacred hour."

Kamenwati placed her hand into the cauldron. Removing it, black liquid dripped from her fingertips. She turned away, and flicked her hand, the black concoction splashed against the invisible fabric of this dimension, and the next.

Rafaela observed curiously from behind, and on the opposite side of the altar.

"Sei." She spoke in Italian as she scribed the number six in the fabric. "Sei." She scribed another symbol. "Sei." Kamenwati scribed a third, and final, six. "By Osiris, and Persephone, give to me your blessing." Beseeching the Egyptian deities of darkness, she asked for their assistance in her dark ritual, and began her spell. "Dark and deep, blacker than hell, cold enough for phantoms to dwell. Accept our sacrifice, and pardon our path, send to us the Phantom glass."

The fabric of reality began to twist, and churn, until a silver substance slithered out. It reached up high, halted, created a corner, and crossed to the right. It halted, created a second corner; repeating the process until four points, and a frame were made. The churning inside flashed, and manifested out of thin air. Lightning struck at it several times until a mirrored surface filled the void. *The Phantom Glass.*

Chapter Thirteen

WHERE IS MY SON? – PART TWO

It was night time in Treadwell, and a warm February breeze caressed the city. A blue mystical energy; accompanied by a gentle tune, floated throughout the streets; hypnotizing, and soothing those struggling to cope with the sudden burst of warmth in the departure of the supernatural storm brought about by Pilar, and her coven connecting with the Hellmouth a few days ago.

Lines of clear light bulbs were strung across the Treadwell Parade Grounds. The theme this year was the 1960s.

Attending the Solstice Gala, mortals danced to the songs performed by the girl band, *Siren Sorority*, on the large circular stage. This was one of the many events open to the public, which takes place during the festival month in the city.

The girl band performed their version of *Anyone Who Had a Heart.* Members Akira, Clartra, Lark, Donovan, and Ryanne were positioned around the edge of the stage with Tigris performing main vocals in the elevated centre. She was a phenomenal soprano. Absent leader Lana (Louisiana) Pratt was M.I.A after leaving some weeks ago to search for missing member Rubella, who was last seen by Connemara Penthal fending off the Sabarticar Demon.

Unseen to the mortals who slow danced around the stage; the magical Sirens were deliberately using their powers to lure evil to them. Watermelon, and purple energy washed over everything, carried by the gentle breeze it was spread as far as Logan Square. But what were they trying to seduce out into the open? Reaching the peak of the chorus, Tigris, who had been singing with her eyes shut, slowly reopened them, and noticed Brady Romani standing among the dancing couples. He raised a finger to his lips. She nodded as she continued to sing; closing her eyes. When she reopened them she found he had disappeared.

Addison Romani, with her beautiful long blonde hair was turned by her male partner as they danced. Her summer dress floated around her knees. Dantalian Romani stood at the bar, and talked to guy named Kad who he had been seeing on, and off for a couple of weeks.

~*~

The city of Treadwell was built in two subdivisions. North Treadwell, on the northern side of the Viridian River, was predominately a residential precinct within the parklands and boasted the cities Children's Hospital. This part of Treadwell was composed of heritage listed homes, and buildings. On the southern side of the river were the CBD's retail, restaurant, and financial districts. On the grassy south bank of the Viridian River – in the distance, the music overpowered the noise of the humans. The light created by lamps glittered across the scales of several black reptiles as they slithered from the dark water. Enjoying the night out, a male, and female, seeking the privacy of the dark, laid on the grass as they lovingly kissed one another. Slithering up the grass, a long black serpent climbed the male's leg.

The man gasped, jumped back and shook his leg. "Ugh, what is that?"

"What is it?" the woman asked before laughing. "You're not caught in the reeds, are you?" She rolled her eyes, and clicked her tongue sarcastically before reaching down, and assisting him.

"Ouch," she shrieked, swiftly pulling her arm, and hand back. "I think it bit me."

Screaming in horror, the man shielded his face with his arms as a large, red belly-black snake lunged at his face. It struck repeatedly, killing him instantly while other snakes bit him all over his body.

Terrified for her life, the woman jumped to her feet. Screaming, she ran into the middle of Viridian Drive which separated her from the help of mortals at the Summer Gala in the Parade Grounds directly opposite. The street was lined with parked cars, but there was no one within hearing distance.

"HELP ME!" she cried frantically.

Slithering quickly through the grass, several black, red bellied snakes massed together. Rising up on the footpath, they assumed a humanoid figure with piercing snake eyes. She blended in with the dark with her skimpy clothing. Extending her arm, she aimed her hand at the mortal woman.

The snake woman hissed, "Intertwine, venom of mine, coursing through this prey, stiffen the spine."

Emitting a blood curdling scream, the mortal woman's spine cracked, she stiffened and froze in the middle of the road.

The serpent accelerated forward until she was flush against her victim. She arched her head to the side, and kissed the woman's neck.

"Scream, call out for someone. Oh, but you can't because you're paralysed. Slither, my master, said I could go out and play." Opening her mouth, thin snake fangs dripped venom. With a demonic growl, she plunged into her victim's neck, killing her instantly as the venom coursed through her veins. "Worthless. I've had better," she complained before flinging the dead woman to the bitumen road.

On the footpath, on the opposite side of the street, Madelyn Romani, accompanied by Dantalian, and Addison, appeared.

Addison was the first to speak, chanting the verse of the vanquishing spell. "Serpent, slither, silent killer. Hunt by heat, striking fast, bind your prey, and paralyse last."

Her body stiffened, and the female serpent demon hissed out a piercing scream to alert others of her kind in the area that she was being attacked by Romani, and to flee.

Dantalian spoke the next verse. "Wither, slight, no venom, nor might."

Madelyn finished with, "Suffer bitch, on thy own venom." She threw a small potion vial containing a green liquid. Smashing against the serpent demon's clothes, she screamed, and was vanquished in a small eruption of flames.

Addison spat impatiently, "Now, we draw out Slither."

Dantalian frowned. "Her scream would have alerted him. If he was here, he would try to return to the Underworld via Logan Square. Draw on the power of the Hellmouth to transport him back."

~*~

B lending into one another, a boy band, known as Riptide – a group of male Sirens – hurried onto the stage as the girls departed. They performed their version of the hit, *Born to Hand Jive,* in blue blazers, pants, and button up shirts. The crowd went wild with freestyle dancing.

Gathering backstage in the tent, Tigris became flustered as her fellow Sirens encroached on her personal space. She spoke frantically, "He was here. I saw Brady Romani in the crowd. It would have to have been an astral projection though, Morgan wouldn't be stupid enough to allow him to flee."

"We don't know that. The night has just started; we will keep using our powers to lure someone from her party here. Capture them. We can play nice or..." Akira said.

Ryanne argued, "Play nice? I think not. I say we butcher the bastards. Better yet, make them sing like a fricken canary."

Returning to the doorway of the tent, the Sirens watched Riptide perform.

Standing on the outside of the dance area near the stage, unnoticed, although in plain sight, a hooded black figure observed the mortals. A forked snake tongue flickered out in and out. Taking into account the height, and build, it appeared to be male in gender. Hearing the scream of the serpent demon before she was vanquished, the hooded figure's head lifted and he walked swiftly toward the exit doors of the gala.

On the Gala side of the entry, a luminescent green glow emanated between two light poles. Drawing on the photons, the green mass grew in strength, until darker green wisps of energy circled up from the ground. In a flash of light, Serene Rein appeared. Her manifestation was invisible to mortals, but visible to the cloaked individual. She levitated above the ground with her organza gown, and long blonde hair floating about her. Her eyes burned an intimidating emerald green.

Revealing a tiny sample of her immense power; tree roots were ripped from the ground. Serene held her hands out at each side gathering light into them. "Children of the earth, powers of the Romani rise. Strength of nature that is mine by rite, I summon you. Power of the earth, bend to me."

Halting, before retaliating, the hooded figure reached its right arm forward and projected venom.

Extending her arm, Serene manipulated the poisonous substance in the air. Once halted, and hovering, she crafted it into a sphere. "I am Serene Rein, Queen, of the Autumn Elves."

The sphere of green venom evaporated.

The figure hissed beneath its hood. "Does it look like I care, because I don't."

Serene gritted her teeth at his blatant lack of respect for higher powers, and instructed the tree roots to surge forward, and bind him. Around his legs, and arms, the roots gripped tight, and immobilized him. She studied him curiously, there was something intriguing about him, something unexplainable.

Serena spat nastily, conjuring light into her hands. "Where is my brother? Where is Brady? Personally, I have no issue in sending you back to Morgana. Piece by piece." There was a protective side to Serena when it came to her family.

With a loud hiss, the cloak the individual was wearing, slipped out of the tree root binds, and crumpled into a heap. He had disappeared. Serene watched curiously.

Rising up in a circular motion, a large anaconda head slithered out of the black. He had assumed his Therianthrope form.

Protecting herself, Serene expanded the light she had conjured into her hands, and created a magical barrier.

The large anaconda hissed as it spoke, "Your power is miniscule, dear niece."

With the mention of the word, niece, Serene immediately made the connection. Slither, in his Anaconda form, held its large eyes level with Serene's as he stood just a few inches away, trying to intimidate her. "Tell mother, if Morgana doesn't kill the boy. I will devour him." He turned, and slithered away in a hurry through the crowd heading for the tree line perimeter. The tree roots conjured, and manipulated by the beautiful blonde Romani, dissolved into the ground as she released them from her control.

Running through the crowd, Addison, Madelyn, and Dantalian halted to regain their breath. Observing a grim looking Serene approaching them, Madelyn remained silent, but was curious.

"What happened?" Dan asked.

Addison asked, "Why did you let him escape?"

Madelyn stepped forward, and calmed her siblings. She then carefully questioned her older sister. "Serene, what was it? What's wrong?"

Serene replied vaguely, as she struggled to comprehend everything, "Slither. He-he is uncle Sheppard, I'm certain of it. He assumed the form of an Anaconda." The two sisters exchanged an uncertain stare. Her younger siblings raised their eyebrows in disbelief.

~*~

Slithering with haste between the trees, Slither, also known as, Sheppard Romani, in his Therianthrope form rose up, and resumed his human figure beneath a heavy cloak. Stepping from the garden, he moved south down Viridian Drive toward Norvard Boulevard. His heavy shadow slithered across the redbrick wall to his immediate left. Suddenly he was grabbed on the arm, he stopped and glanced to his right as a homeless man spoke to him.

"Do you have any weed man?"

Hissing viciously at the innocent mortal man, Sheppard lunged at his neck, biting him, and killing him instantly with his poisonous venom. Pulling away he shoved the dead man to the ground, and carried on his way. Crossing the street, and moving out from the cover of the trees, he became visible to a large creature flying overhead. A few seconds later, making its presence felt, its call sang like a bird of prey. Feeling threatened, Sheppard came to a stop in the middle of the street. He turned his head left, and right, before looking up. Dismissing his fear, he hurriedly ventured across the intersection of Norvard Boulevard, completely ignoring the pedestrian crossing which flashed red.

A grainy mist descended on Viridian Drive, and with a whoosh, a large Griffin – head, talons, and large wings of an eagle, and body of a lion – landed. Its piercing hawk eyes gleamed with the glow of the street lights as it eagerly watched Slither disappear down the small street on the opposite side of the road. Impatiently it flapped its large wings, rose up onto its hind legs, and took flight again. In the seclusion of the night sky, it called to its kin, and four other distinct silhouettes flew across the sky toward him.

Hurrying along Gawler Place, Sheppard turned his head every so often, glancing fearfully over his shoulder for anyone who looked suspicious. Yet, he was the evil one. Looking for suspicious individuals was rather ironic. Ahead of him was Treadwell City Mall; he could disappear into the shadows, and return to the evil city of Eris where Morgana awaited his return. A whooshing noise overhead caused him to halt. Looking ahead, he saw the dark shadow of a winged creature cross over the shop fronts of City Mall.

Like a snake he hissed, and his snake eyes shone beneath the hood of his cloak.

Swooping down, a woman flapping large brown eagle wings lowered to the ground. Her hair was long, golden blonde with streaks of brown and her wings turned into humanoid arms. She wore a white vest of feathers, golden brown long sleeve shirt, brown pants, and camel coloured boots.

Genvera was the leader of her group of Griffins. They had migrated to Treadwell from the Delamere Forest, Cheshire, in North West England. Drawn by the power of the Hellmouth, it enhanced their strength tenfold. Just like bird of prey would fly over, and swoop down on small and unsuspecting creatures; the

Griffins did the same to evil individuals. They could smell the evil of Sheppard/Slither.

She spoke with a thick British accent, "I could smell your stench a mile away, you have something which does not belong to you. With a swing of her of her arm, she fired brown feathers, cleverly made of metal, and sharp as knives, at him.

He hissed and projected venom from his mouth, melting the approaching attack.

With another swing of her arm, but this time gesturing her hand as well, she fired a bolt of light at the venomous snake. Striking him with the power, she stunned him. She had rendered him unconscious, and he fell to the ground. She approached, and glared down on him with great despise in her hawk eyes.

"Traitor," she spat.

~*~

Sheppard opened his eyes some hours later, and noticed wooden floorboards. They were cold against his cheek. Lifting his head, he looked about, an unpleasant feeling consumed him as he immediately acknowledged his new surroundings. He was lying on the floor, of the gloomy Romani attic. His eyes flicked from left to right as he inspected the room for hidden company. Rising to his feet, he attempted to step forward, but was thrown back by a powerful and invisible force. Around him, five crystals reacted; flashing white, remaining aglow as he levitated back up onto his feet.

Pilar revealed her presence as the gloomy light brightened. "Welcome, Sheppard." She was not alone. Siobhan, Julianne, Zane, and Ryder Romani, were in her company along with Renae, and Basset; the families Custodians.

Pilar's voice became firm and unforgiving. "Your stay here will not be friendly. Let me be crystal clear and I speak for the others, you're no brother of ours. You're a traitor."

Reacting to her insulting words, he shapeshifted into his anaconda form, and his height shifted from six feet tall to a towering nine feet. He hissed at his sister nastily, and swiftly struck with his fangs drawn.

RETURN OF THE GAMMA WITCH – PART TWO

The attic of Aaron Pogue's house was gloomy. In the centre of the room a black smoke swirled in a circle, before rising swiftly. Reaching the height of six feet as it spun, arms clad in a baggy cloak reached out, at the ends, withered hands with long fingers. Beneath its hood, once it stopped rotating, eerie blue glowing eyes became evident.

In a corner by the window, Isadora jolted a rod in her hand. Mechanically, it extended into a bow with a line of ultra-violet light. Pulling back, an arrow of light manifested. She released it, firing an attack at the demon. Isadora Pogue was a proficient markswoman, when it came to archery she always hit her targets without hassle. Sometimes with her eyes shut.

Emitting a hostile scream, the cloaked fiend swiftly moved an arm out in front. Deflecting the arrow, it sent it telekinetically at Bermuda Pogue directly across the room.

She stood with her arm extended, her hand rigid. Exhibiting a golden glow, she utilized her power of Deflection to redirect it back at the evil fiend.

Screaming again, the hooded figure extended its arm and halted the arrow in mid-air. The demon spoke with a croaky old woman's voice, "such pretty powers for pretty witches. I love devouring pretty witches " Removing its hood, an ugly hag was revealed. Hideous looking would be a compliment in this case.

Bermuda huffed and blew stray locks of hair from her face. "Isadora, blind her." It was indicated she was in charge of the situation. "It's time we vanquished the old broad."

Lowering her bow to her side, Isadora extended her other arm, and using her power of Photokinesis, caused the still arrow of light to explode with a blinding flash.

Abiteth, the Devourer, was a hag. The Pogue Book of Shadows stipulates she is a devourer of the beautiful. Drawn to bedazzling powers such as Photokinesis, and beautiful creatures like Wood Nymphs, Fairies and Good Witches, Abiteth feeds on her victims to extend her already long life, and restore her youth to hide her ugly form. Blinding her will only last a few moments before her scream will disorientate you.

Struck in the back, Abiteth shrieked and fell to the floor.

Andromeda emerged gallant, marvelling in her achievement. Her blonde hair was pulled back in a ponytail revealing a graze on her cheek where she had been thrown against the wall by Abiteth. She summoned her sisters, "Quickly, blinding her will only last a few seconds. Do you have the vanquishing spell?"

Isadora pulled a piece of paper from her back pocket, and handed it to her.

Andromeda spoke the first verse, "Beautiful born, a blessing, and adorn."

"Devour to hide your ugly form," said Isadora.

Bermuda continued, "vanquished now, none shall mourn."

With the conclusion of the spell, Abiteth, as she lay on the floor, let out a scream. Flames ravaged her body, and she was vanquished, leaving only a black mark on the floor.

Raising her eyes, Isadora looked across at Andromeda cautiously. "Shane."

Leaving the attic in a flurry, Bermuda, Andromeda, and Isadora filed down the staircase to the second storey of the house. Halting before the ajar bedroom door, Isadora watched her sister disappear along the hallway, and down the staircase to the ground floor. Approaching the bedroom door, she carefully pushed it open, and peered inside the dark room. Startled, she gasped as a little boy, not much older than three moved into the light shining in from the hallway.

"Bunny," she used his pet name, pulling him to her as she picked him up. "What are you doing?" Pushing the door open, she entered the gloomy room. "Why aren't you in bed?"

"Was she a bad lady, mama?"

She appeared awkward as she stared at his little face with blue eyes and topped with blonde hair. She brushed the locks from his face as she tucked him back into bed. Isadora felt compelled to teach her young son the ways of the world, the good, and the bad in it, and its endless possibilities; but that would lead to more questions than understanding. So, she left the question unanswered, and smiled.

"Owen, you were a good boy. You behave like a good boy should." Isadora turned her head, and looked across the room, noticing Owen's twin brother, Lyndon asleep in his bed. "She wasn't very nice."

His curious eyes settled, he yawned, and turned over in his bed.

"Sleep well, Bunny."

"I love you mama."

Isadora smiled as her tough heart softened, "I love you too."

She moved from the bed, and crossed to where her other son, Lyndon slept. She leant down, kissed him on his head, pulled his blankets up, and left the room. Behind the door, a ghostly mist gathered and Aaron Pogue appeared.

~*~

On the floor in the lounge room, unconscious, and bleeding from wounds covered by his clothes, Shane lay in the ruin of the glass, and timber coffee table.

Hours prior to her vanquish, Abiteth had been drawn to the house after being ambushed by Andromeda, Bermuda, Isadora, and Shane, in Treadwell Botanical Gardens. She'd been attacking mortals across the city who she deemed beautiful, and pretty to feed on.

The girls hurried down the stairs, Andromeda in front, Bermuda behind, and halted at the doorway to observe for a moment. As they entered into the room, a swirl of black smoke rose up from the floor. Rising up tall, arms extended out, withered hands slipped out of the baggy sleeves, and eerie, vicious eyes beamed out from beneath a hood.

"INDY!" Bermuda yelled.

Andromeda glared in disgust. "You've got to be kidding me."

Retaliating, Abiteth let out a scream.

Grabbing their ears, the twins buckled in agony as they became disorientated by the vocal power of the evil fiend.

"Fools." Abiteth lowered to Shane. "You should read your precious book meticulously instead of looking down your nose at it." She touched his face tenderly before she would feed on his life-force. "I am Abiteth, the Devourer. I did not get my name by chance. It came with reputation. It takes four sibling witches to vanquish me, not three."

Skidding to a halt at the doorway on the opposite side of the room, Isadora, with a cold glare brought her arms up quickly and flicked her hands. Using her power of Energy Manipulation, she blasted Abiteth, throwing her backward into the fireplace.

Isadora screamed, "GET UP, GET UP NOW, BEFORE SHE DOES." Swinging her arm, she used her offensive power to throw Abiteth as she rose, across the room and over the lounge. "Get Shane."

Andromeda and Bermuda did as commanded, allowing Isadora to take charge. "Wake him up, we're going to need him in vanquishing the demon."

Fearful, Andromeda cried, "he's bleeding, if he is not healed, he will die, Indy." She removed her hand from his back to notice it covered in blood. "We need Prid," she named their newly appointed Custodian in Noah's absence, "to heal him."

Isadora stood firm, her indigo coloured eyes a deep purple as she watched Abiteth rise from behind the lounge "Bring him here, if we hold his hand, we'll be able to channel his power. Then we say the spell, vanquish her for good and we call...."

Bermuda cried out, "PRID, WE NEED YOU. SHANE IS HURT."

Andromeda, and Bermuda, with an unconscious Shane moved quickly across the room to where Isadora's stood.

Isadora shook her head, "You yelled loud enough that the whole neighbourhood can hear you." Her sisters, and Shane stood silently at her side. Ahead she watched a vile, and pissed off Abiteth move into the middle of the room. "Let's go bitch."

Throwing her hood back, and revealing her hideous visage, the evil fiend used her powers to scream, and disorientate her victims.

Isadora held her arm forward. gestured her hand. Using her power of Energy Manipulation, she blasted her opponent in the mouth, obliterating her voice box. "That ought to shut you up," she said sarcastically. "Grab Shane's hands." She took Bermuda's hand. "Beautiful born, a blessing and adorn."

"Devour to hide your ugly form," said Andromeda.

Bermuda added, "vanquished now, none shall mourn."

Throwing her arms about as she arched her back, Abiteth screamed in agony, and with the power of the four witches was permanently vanquished in a fiery explosion.

Hearing Shane groan in pain at her feet, Bermuda brushed her long hair back from her face, gazed at him tenderly, and raised her eyes to the ceiling.

"For god sake, PRIDHAM."

A spiral of white smoke rose from the floor, and a woman appeared. Long brunette hair, amethyst coloured eyes, and dressed in white and grey clothes.

"About fricken time, where have you been? Learning to fly by the seat of your pants?" Andromeda grumbled.

Pridham, their female Custodian apologized. "Forgive me, I only just heard your call. For some reason, it is not strong enough in this house. Something here weakens it."

Isadora's scrutinizing eyes softened as she observed the woman. Judging by her body language, and pout, Pridham was telling the truth.

The Custodian ignored Andromeda's bitchy attitude.

Isadora fixed her eyes on the woman across the room. "Never mind, we need you to heal Shane. He is hurt pretty bad."

Pridham hurried across the room.

Catching a glimpse of something out of the ordinary, Bermuda noticed a man who looked very similar to Aaron Pogue standing by the mirror on the wall beside the doorway. He simply stared at its reflective surface; lost in a daze of himself looking back.

"What...?" she murmured to herself curiously.

Kneeling down beside her charge as he lay on the floor, Pridham placed her hands at the top of his head, before slowly moving them down the length of his arms, torso and body, until down to his feet with a subtle glow beneath them. Stirring, and becoming fully conscious again, Shane arched his back, gasped, and threw himself into a sitting position.

The sound of the front door opening was heard. Andromeda looked across and her eyes were the first to catch a glimpse of Aaron Pogue, and Ravenna returning from their night out. Acknowledging her parents, Bermuda moved her gaze to where the man had stood before the mirror only to notice he had already disappeared.

"What happened?" Ravenna asked, acknowledging the broken coffee table. "Uninvited guest?" Turning, she greeted the Custodian in the room, her small eyes held a hint of despise in them. "Hello Pridham, you can go now."

Pridham, doing as she was told, nodded and departed, teleporting in a brisk swirl of white smoke.

Ravenna sighed happily, and touched her hair for a moment.

"You're home early, how was the Solstice Gala?"" Isadora tried to make her voice sound calm as she avoided her mother's initial question."

An obnoxious Andromeda revealed, "We had a demon attack here. Tempest transported Perry and Noah away for their own safety. The four of us vanquished Abiteth."

Ravenna, and Aaron appeared calm, but it was clear they were annoyed.

Ravenna spoke telepathically to Aaron, and formed a smile to deter her children. "I thought you said they could not access that level of power?"

Aaron replied telepathically, "Hmm..."

Observing inconspicuously, Bermuda listened in on the thoughts being exchanged.

Moving her eyes down, a red colour on Aaron's hand, he thought he'd carefully hidden, caught her attention. *Blood, she thought to herself?*

~*~

High above the world, within its magical dimension, lay a grassy plateau – magically removed from the earth below – heavily forested with Amabalis fir, Arbutus, Black Cottonwood, Douglas-fir, Mountain hemlock, Sitka spruce, Western hemlock, Western red-cedar. Secretly a Hellmouth, and unlike others around the globe, it did not settle properly into the earth's foundations. It was equal in size to Stanley Park in British Columbia. Seeing the potential to use its ultimate power for good, the Glacier Castle was built upon it. It became a place for teaching generations of witches under the command of Queen Maria of Good Magic.

The colossal castle made of glacier ice stood in the spotlight of the moon's glow. The trees were elegantly lit with the twinkling light of fireflies. Their amber glow captured an unlikely creature; a winged cougar, feather and fur normally ash grey as it flew between the trees toward an unknown destination. A kind nature revealed in its amethyst coloured eyes.

At the edge of the plateau, overlooking the human world below, and hidden amongst the forest, was a beautiful roman amphitheatre. Around the ground level were white stone columns. The steps down led to a circular standing area where a large golden orb levitated, its liquid surface shimmered, and swayed. In three individual beams of white light, three women appeared in Grecian gowns. They were Oracles of Phaedra.

A blonde-haired Oracle spoke, "greetings, my liege." She lowered her head at Maria as a sign of respect. "Blessed are we to have you in our place of worship."

Standing at the foot of the steps, Maria stood stiffly, her arms folded, eyes closed as she cleared her mind. Her long blonde hair hung over her right shoulder. She wore a knitted vest over a purple satin blouse, and grey suit pants. At her side, white smoke spiralled up, and in a golden glow which followed, the CEO of the Government Supernatural Bureau, and Maria's husband manifested. He stood just as powerful, dressed in a crisp grey business suit. His styled brown hair glistened in the moonlight.

He asked, "why?"

Maria indicated for her husband to stay silent while she closed her eyes and listened for the approaching winged cougar. Swooping from between the tree trunks on the ground level of the amphitheatre, the magical beast flew overhead before landing. Two more flew from the forest, and circled overhead.

The CEO glanced up as his attention was grabbed by the creatures before turning back to his wife.

When she opened her eyes, they turned from humble brown to a striking blue with fiery power. Her hair floated above and her aura danced with visible energy. Calming herself, and her power, the visible magic lessened and her hair curled back over her shoulder.

Pridham, the female Custodian of the Pogue Witches descended the steps. She stopped to catch her breath as she reached the open area. Panic was present in her voice when she spoke. "My queen, I bring you information." She greeted her superior, the CEO, with a nod.

On the top level, Renae Ketch, and her husband Basset appeared.

Maria politely addressed the brunette woman before her, "you may speak Pridham. What news do you bring of the Pogue Witches?"

Renae and Basset moved alongside the CEO.

Pridham began nervously, fearing her assumption could be misplaced. "I fear there is an evil in Summit Hills."

Renae, as a seasoned Custodian herself, saw Pridham as new and inexperienced. "I think it's everywhere, Pridham. It's not really an isolated anomaly. You are new to the code, you'll get a better gauge of it over time."

Pridham's amethyst eyes narrowed, and she growled like a cougar. "I will be more specific. I fear there is an evil in Aaron Pogue's house. I was barely able to hear Bermuda's call to heal Shane." The two Old Ones listened with concern. "Something is trying to block us from them."

Renae seemed more apologetic now, and less judgemental toward Pridham. "Speaking of evil, Pilar and the Triad joined forces with Genvera of the Griffins to capture Slither, one of Morgana's cronies. Do we have the G.S.B deal with this? Or let them, vanquish him?"

The CEO, and Maria exchanged a look of uncertainty.

~*~

*H*ours earlier, in downtown Treadwell, telling their children

they had attended the Solstice Gala; Aaron and Ravenna stood in a dingy alleyway opposite an individual dressed in a trench coat. It was too dark to make out any distinct facial features, but it appeared to be male when taking into account, the broadness of his shoulders.

"How did it feel this time?" he asked.

At Aaron's feet lay a deceased mortal, whom he had butchered with the blood-soaked knife in his right hand. What possessed him to go to such lengths as to become a murderer? Aaron grinned, revelling in the pleasure of both the hunt, and kill.

Ravenna spoke confidently, "we can guarantee Perry and Noah are trapped."

"And how does the boss know for sure?" the shady male asked. "Your word means nothing if you have no solid evidence."

Aaron growled, insulted. "You dare doubt us?"

The man continued in a firmer voice. "The boss does, you know the game. You were to trap him in the mirror, and set up the witches. Bermuda will bring them back. Then you convince them to reconnect with the Sundial so we can steal their joint power."

Aaron spat, "and, how do you suppose we get her to do that? I renounced all magic, all my powers. Do you think she will take orders from someone who dislikes her practicing witchcraft?"

The man roared, "FIGURE IT OUT!" He vanished, teleporting away in a fiery combustion.

~*~

Returning to the attic upstairs, Andromeda entered the room first, followed by Bermuda, Isadora, Shane, Aaron, and Ravenna. Halting in the gloomy room, lit by soft burning lampshades mounted on the walls, they were greeted by a different Gamma Witch other than the testy Tempest Pogue. In the middle of the room, standing within a circle of white flame lit candles with Noah and Perry on either side of her, Philomena Beaumont appeared much calmer, and more approachable than her older sister.

"Tempest said she'd return with their bodies when..." Andromeda's voice dropped out mid-speech, and she queried cautiously, "Who-who, who are you?" She lifted her arm, and pointed at the witch before her. "Are you friend, or foe?"

The two had never met before. Philomena had only ever met Bermuda, Isadora, and Shane on her previous visit at a different location. Philomena stood silently. "I am...." she began.

Bermuda interrupted, and moved around her sister, halting in front of the small assembly. "Philomena Beaumont! You're Tempest's sister. Why are you here? Where is Tempest?"

Philomena smiled, complimented by the young witch's uncanny memory. She lifted her arms, and placed her hands in one another. "There is no need for pleasantries. I am here on your grandmother/great-grandmother's behalf. She had to stay behind to tend to some pressing issues."

Isadora asked with confusion, "what kind of pressing issues could affect the dead?"

Chapter Fifteen

TO LIMBO....

Heavy, smothering shadows clung to three of the four walls of Rafaela's lair. Within them, demons and evil entities lingered. They would wait until their master summoned one or they presented themselves in the middle of the open floor where she would give, or they would offer, their powers to attack a witch or mortal. Sitting on her throne, legs crossed, one arm folded across her waist, the other bent up, Rafaela rested her hand against her porcelain cheek, and curiously gazed upon the ocean floor on the other side of the colossal window to her left.

Slipping out of the shadows, a beautiful, beguiling woman with long teal hair down to her waist, and dressed in a roman gown, showed herself. Her voice had a sweet tone when she spoke. "You need inspiring, may I be of service? I am Melpomene, Muse of Tragedy."

Rafaela wriggled in her seat, curiosity rose in her face, and she smirked. "You're one of the nine Muse Queens. Abiteth, the Devourer failed. So, what can a Muse offer me?"

Melpomene, excited to prove herself, rushed forward in a blur. "Let me go into Limbo. I'd love to play with Noah and Perry. Let me inspire them to crossover to the other side. It would be such a tragedy, the most powerful line of witches dying before their power can be reconstituted."

~*~

Downstairs in her kitchen, sipping at a mug of hot tea; Pilar Romani telekinetically turned pages as she read the articles in her WitchCraft Magazine. Perhaps she read it to see what was being said about her son's disappearance, who knows? Or, maybe rumours about the evil witch Morgana, or mortal world gossip.

The eldest sister, Siobhan entered the room with a hint of frustration in her voice. "He isn't going to talk, Pilar. No matter what we say or do to him."

Pilar lifted her head, turning her attention to her sister.

"I don't know how I feel about using the Truth Spell on him." Siobhan continued.

Pilar hissed nastily. "he's a snake. I personally hate the garden variety. But, him," she gestured to the ceiling. "I intend on making his stay here one he'll remember in life, and in the next one."

Siobhan leant against the kitchen counter as she observed her bitter sister.

"You do not assist in the abduction of my son, and brush it off with a smile. Sorry, not me. His betrayal is his demise, and that demise will be at my hands."

Siobhan retorted, "if a higher power doesn't get in first."

"Maria?" As Pilar replied her Smartphone began to ring, and vibrate on the counter next to her mug. "One second, sorry." Placing the device to her ear, she listened, and replied with, "Okay, no worries. I'll be there shortly," and hung up.

Siobhan asked, "Everything okay?"

Pilar responded as she slid from the barstool. ""Bermuda Pogue. It seems the Gamma Witches have returned. They need my help."

"Help with what, may I ask?" Siobhan appeared cautious now.

Pilar replied as she walked away, "we channelled the power of the Hellmouth, remember? They want to do the same thing to bring Noah and Perry back from where ever it is they are trapped."

Siobhan nodded.

Entering the attic some moments later, Pilar approached Sheppard, and closed the door behind her. Its outline gave off a glow, magically sealing itself to prevent his escape. He sat tied to a chair in the middle of the room, five crystals surrounded him; should he move he'd cause them to react, and generate a force field powerful enough to incapacitate him. Standing by the window Zane, and Juliann guarded their guest prisoner.

Pilar kept fierce eye contact with her brother. "I've got some business to attend to, so I'm leaving you in the capable care of these two." She turned to her other siblings. "Try not to kill him, I'd like a piece."

Observing her as she stood in front of him, Sheppard became uneasy when Morgana manifested in Pilar's Silhouette. Her eyes were completely white, complimented by long, wiry grey hair, gaunt cheeks, grey lips, and as she growled at him revealed jagged shark-like teeth. Pilar turned her head slightly, and her eyes gleamed with the lustrous idea that he feared her.

"I'll be going now," Pilar said before leaving the room.

A second ghost circled Sheppard's prison, "Tsk. Tsk. Tsk," she clicked her tongue. Typhoid was as beautiful as she was evil, dressed in knee high, suede boots, short gypsy skirt, corset, and black lace gloves reaching to her elbows. "Sheppard, Sheppard, Sheppard." She used her powers to manipulate his body, and turned his head against his will toward her. "Aren't you the stupid idiot?"

He wanted to speak, but she clenched his throat with her magic. He gulped uneasily.

"Don't fret your knickers, they can't see us. We're invisible to them. What's the matter?" She tilted her head to one side, a manic gleam in her eyes. She barked, "cat got your tongue? "

~*~

The attic of Aaron Pogue's Summit Hills home was well lit now when compared to its gloomy state earlier when Philomena Beaumont had arrived, returning Noah and Perry's bodies to the human world. Directly in the middle of the room, surrounded by a large circle of white candles, their bodies lay in comfortable slumber. Or, so it seemed.

Aaron and Ravenna stood on the far side of the room, the moon's glow capturing them as it shone in through the window. The shadows created great lines in their faces which made them appear even more untrustworthy.

In the middle of the room, toward one wall Isadora, Shane, Andromeda, and Philomena brewed a concoction in a cauldron on the table they stood around.

Downstairs, Bermuda ended her phone call to Pilar Romani as she paced the dining room of the house. From the corner of her eye, something caught her attention, and she halted in her tracks near the twelve-seater table. She turned to find a man with shaggy, sandy blonde locks, dressed in jeans, shirt, and blazer, in the lounge room.

Carefully, and quietly, she approached the doorway, and stopped. Pressing two fingers to the left side of her temple, she attempted to use the telepathy branch of her Sensazione power to listen in on his thoughts. She needed to figure if he was friend or foe. She'd seen him multiple times now, and always in the same spot, observing the bloody mirror like his life depended on it.

"I realize now," he spoke aloud.

Bermuda's eyebrows rose when she realized he must have been talking to her. "Pardon me?" she replied uneasily. Carefully she slipped away from the doorframe of the archway leading into the lounge room, and crossed to the middle of the room. "Do I know you?"

There was a knock at the front door.

Bermuda called out while keeping eye contact with the man in front of her. "Hello? Who is it?"

"It's me. Pilar."

"Come in, Pilar, the door is unlocked."

The front door opened, and Pilar Romani entered, closing the door behind her. She noted the hallway ahead, and an imposing staircase on the left. Hearing a male's voice to her immediate right, she entered what was the lounge room.

"Aaron," she greeted the man. Glancing to her left, she acknowledged an extremely spooked, Bermuda Pogue. "Have I come at a bad time?"

An intrigued Bermuda asked, "Whoa. Wait. What? Who did you just say?" She hurried across the room to the doorway opposite Pilar. Turning toward the man, she acknowledged his true identity. "Aaron?" She peered up at the ceiling, wondering who was in the attic with her siblings. "How are you a ghost?"

Pilar spoke with obvious confusion, "Hold on, I can see him, how can he be a ghost?"

"I think I'm the only one who can see him." Bermuda turned, and headed for the staircase. "Come. I want to show you something really creepy."

Pilar followed without hesitation, and the ghost of Aaron disappeared into the mirror.

~*~

T he door to the attic swung open when Bermuda turned, and pushed against the handle.

Pilar followed her in. She observed the occupants in the room, and noted Aaron standing by the window with Ravenna. "I see what you mean by creepy," she muttered beneath her breath.

Philomena crossed the room to greet the Romani woman and they exchanged a handshake. "Welcome, Pilar Romani, right? You're the image of Una."

Pilar responded curiously, "you knew my mother?"

Philomena smiled. "Very well. Come." They moved to where Isadora, Andromeda, and Shane stood near a table. "Tell me, my dear. How did you manage to summon the power of the Hellmouth?"

Bermuda observed Ravenna, and Aaron. Their thoughts were silent which was most intimidating for the young witch. If their minds where silent, what were they plotting?

Pilar explained, "the Triad. Firstly, we're the children of earth, whereas you're a child of the divine power. We're able to channel power through Zane, our brother. He is a conduit. The magic passes through him before siphoning into the rest of us. He acts as an anchor to the earth to which we can summon colossal power. Without him we risk killing ourselves. In the days of Treadwell's first settlement, it was the blood of your ancestor, and mine, which closed the Hellmouth."

Philomena was intrigued. Of course, she had heard of their coming as the new breed known as the Mischling. "The Hellmouth is connected to us?"

Pilar's smile implied a lot, from the corner of her eyes, she curiously observed Aaron before answering Philomena. "It tastes like rust. You're a Gamma Witch. How is it you didn't know the Hellmouth was connected to you?"

Philomena suddenly felt extremely uneducated. "Why do I suspect you're going to tell me, the birdbath thing Tempest keeps in her garden, is somehow related to all of this Hellmouth hoo-ha?"

Pilar chuckled. "The birdbath is actually a Sundial. Your family has had that totem of power since before Cleopatra. The Sundial is the key to the Hellmouth, to any Hellmouth in fact. Like our Solar Star Talisman is *our* key. Together, both our covens, being sister traditions, are Treadwell's guard...."

Pilar was cut off midsentence by a loud bang, and flash of light. The concoction which had been brewing was ready. Shane fanned the smoke away from the cauldron. He used a pipette to extract the brown substance, and filled two small potion vials.

Andromeda cringed at the idea of having to drink the disgusting looking liquid. "That looks revolting. Ten bets it tastes like ass. It looks like it does."

Isadora taunted, "You've probably kissed many I imagine."

Andromeda glared at her sister. Lifting the small vials, Shane gave them a few quick shakes until they turned a delightful purple. Moving around the table, she handed one to Bermuda, and the other to Andromeda.

"The potion is ready," he announced with a flourish of his hand.

Andromeda cringed at the idea of drinking the substance, "Why must I do this? Isadora can..." she was cut off midsentence.

Isadora growled, narrowed her eyes and folded her arms. "I am not you're twin, Bermuda is, and we all know your power is amplified when you're together."

Having moved away from the table, Philomena made a protective ring around the outside of the large circle of candles where Noah, and Perry lay.

Stepping into the circle, Pilar knelt down before the two men's heads. "Come on ladies, you asked me here to help you summon the power of the Hellmouth, so let's get cracking. The longer they stay trapped in limbo, the harder it will be to revive them."

Bermuda, and her twin sister gazed at the Romani woman before turning to acknowledge one another with certain signs of concern. Stepping away from the table, the sisters entered the circle. Andromeda knelt down beside Noah, and Bermuda beside Perry. The air rippled slightly, enough for Isadora to notice as the magic within confines of the circle amplified. Spontaneously, flames ignited atop the candles.

Aaron, and Ravenna observed curiously as the glow of the flames glimmered in their cold eyes. He stood stiff with his hands hidden behind his back, a scrutinizing expression on his face. You could see his disgust for witchcraft in the crumpling of his lips.

Bermuda, and Andromeda carefully placed rose petals, sprigs of lavender, and salt over the men's bodies. Upon finishing, they glanced at each another nervously. Raising the potion vials to their lips, they knocked them back in one gulp. Andromeda appeared to savour the taste while her sister did not.

Bermuda cringed. "Bleh, it tastes like ass."

Pilar gazed down at the families open Book of Shadows lying on the floor to her side. The title of the page read: *To Restore One from Darkness.* Holding her arms out in front of her, she tilted her head, eyes closed toward the ceiling and absorbed the surrounding magic.

"Place one of your hands on Noah, and Perry," she instructed the twin witches. "With the other, hold each other's hand. This will keep your power connected, and also connected to the same dimension both of these men are trapped in."

Bermuda, and Andromeda nodded, and interlocked their free hands with one another. Revealing its potency, a magical force manifested with the sister's connection. So powerful, it attempted to force their hands apart, and for a moment gave off a magnificent golden glow.

Pilar lowered her head; her eyes sprang open with a fierce strength captured within them and her hands latched onto Andromeda, and Bermuda's, forearms. The mild, but forceful power she was channeling, was nothing compared to the full force of the Hellmouth.

"Veniat ad me (Come to me)," Pilar chanted in Latin. "Hear my call. I summon power great and old, from this city which is home, only to borrow, not to own."

Seconds passed before a disembodied groan of something massive resonated throughout the house, street, and country town of Summit Hills. Gasping aloud, Bermuda, and Andromeda's eyes were forced shut, and a foreign power surged through their bodies. A white light emanated from Pilar's body.

"Pilar," Isadora cried out in fear,

Approaching the circle with Shane beside her, Isadora, and Shane let out a scream as they were thrown back by an invisible force. A massive, angelic-looking, beastial creature, with an enormous mouth full of jagged teeth emerged from the Romani's body with its open wings, and multiple heads. With a heavy thud, Shane slammed against the wall, and Isadora crashed into a wardrobe which collapsed under her impact.

The personification of the Hellmouth let out an earth-shaking roar, and in an instant disappeared. Returning to Pilar before being passed on to Bermuda, and Andromeda, who both let out agonizing screams.

The sisters cast the *To Restore One from Darkness* spell. "Hear now the prayer of light, may it call to you in still of night. Victims who have fallen into blight, we restore you back to the world of light."

Standing across the other side of the room, behind his back, Aaron fiddled with a small pink crystal he had cleverly hidden up his sleeve. He curiously watched the two witches, and Pilar perform the spell to bring his brothers back. From the corner of his eye, he noticed Isadora climbing out of the rubble of the wardrobe brushing herself off before she tended to Shane. He saw an opportunity.

"Expergisci, (Awaken)" Aaron murmured in Latin.

The crystal in his hand gave off a subtle glow, and below the two sister witches, Perry Pogue's eyes suddenly opened with an evident evil in them as they gasped, and plunged into Limbo.......

TO BE CONTINUED......

ABOUT THE AUTHOR

I hail from Adelaide, South Australia, home of the renowned Barossa Valley and McLaren Vale Wines.

My humble city is also the murder capital of Australia.

I love all things fantasy. As a child, I loved writing short stories, but a passion for writing manifested at a turbulent point in my adolescence. My imagination has me away with the fairies most of the time, wishing I had a super power to triumph over all that is bad in this world. Reality has me working a nine-to-five job.

When I'm away from the computer, I love watching anime, drinking coffee to my heart's content, listening and dancing, around the house to music. I'm a child of the 80's nothing gets my imagination flowing like Bon Jovi.

I believe everyone has a book inside them, it just requires something to bring it to the surface.

SOCIAL LINKS

Website - http://www.trkester.com.au/

Instagram - https://www.instagram.com/t.r.kester/

Facebook - https://www.facebook.com/TRKesterBooks/